W9-BUJ-479

Praise for *(H)afrocentric*

"Smith's comics ooze with originality."
—AFROPUNK

"*(H)afrocentric* is a book that is incredibly contemporary and fits the progressive minds of today's readers. It tackles issues of intersectionality and gentrification in ways that are not only informative but also entertaining. It's unlike any comic book I've ever read."
—Jamie Broadnax, founder and managing editor of Blackgirlnerds.com

"*(H)afrocentric* is fully dope, artistic, brilliantly drawn, styled, and wonderfully radical with an awesomely fiery heroine! Juliana Smith and her team are to be commended for this desperately needed political and cultural contribution. Get into it and grab your soapboxes!"
—Jared A. Ball, author of *I Mix What I Like! A Mixtape Manifesto*

"*(H)afrocentric* is a wonderful continuation of satire within the African American literary tradition. As a comic, its bittersweet and biting social/political commentary picks up where Aaron McGruder's *Boondocks* left off. As an American literary work, Smith echoes the sentiments of her predecessors, such as Ishmael Reed, Marita Bonner, Sherman Alexie, Dorothy Parker, Charles Wright, and George Schuyler, all of whom wittily write about the ironies of Otherness. While it remains to be seen what fate awaits Naima Pepper and company, it is certain that their journey will be filled with much-needed insight and humor."
—Shamika Mitchell, professor of English, Rockland Community College

"*(H)afrocentric* is witty, socially conscious and progressive. It is one of my favorite comics because it gives the reader wit, commentary on current complex social issues, and humor, while depicting a gender-diverse cast of young, educated millennials of color. *(H)afrocentric* is timely as it grapples with current issues such as gentrification, the politics of representation, and race relations. I love the ideologically divergent perspectives of the characters and the multidimensional iconography the comic portrays. It is a must-read!"
—Sheena Howard, coeditor of *Black Comics: Politics of Race and Representation*

Volumes 1–4

(H)afrocentric Comics: Volumes 1–4
© 2017 Juliana "Jewels" Smith and PM Press
All rights reserved.

ISBN: 978-1-62963-448-7
Library of Congress Control Number: 2017942907

Cover by Ronald Nelson and Mike Hampton
Interior design by briandesign

10 9 8 7 6 5 4 3 2 1

PM Press
PO Box 23912
Oakland, CA 94623
www.pmpress.org

Printed in the USA by the Employee Owners of Thomson-Shore in Dexter, Michigan.
www.thomsonshore.com

CONTENTS

Foreword

Kiese Laymon

(H)afrocentric came into my life as I was becoming a contentious, old, crusty-lipped black man who hated all things literary. I was sure that American literary writing and American literary writers were a major part of our American mess. I understood that literature—as potent and transformative as we hoped it was—had not morally transformed our abusive nation. The problem, I thought, was not that books, notes, and stories can't change the world; it's that there are so many books and stories peddling in structural and interpersonal abuse without calling it structural and interpersonal abuse. In my hateful old black man splendor, I argued with anyone who would listen that most books and most book writers had made our nation worse. The architects of this empire, I argued, read and wrote books. They used a lot of words. They told tons of stories. The question was not simply what distinguishes us so-called literary writers from the architects of empire; it was how do we so-called literary writers use our words and white space to undo the massively violent work of the misused words and white space before us.

Then I met and read *(H)afrocentric Volume 2* and I hated a lot less because I saw what I never thought possible. *(H)afrocentric* is a once-in-a-generation liberatory creation that really pushes in ways that are neither precious nor convenient. *(H)afrocentric* is the best of *Boondocks*, without crusty misogynoir. It's the best of Chappelle, without uncritical transphobia. It's the best of *A Different World* and *Atlanta* without commercial breaks every eight minutes selling you colorful sugar and fried meats.

(H)afrocentric uses words, shapes, colors, notes, and queer black American stories to bring more compassion, bluesy craft, and ultimately freedom to white space. With hands that are neither heavy nor telegraphed, *(H)afrocentric* creatively imagines odd characters in need of more loving touch from an absolutely absurd nation.

I was a crusty old black man on the verge of not believing in the power of art anymore. Then I met *(H)afrocentric*. And I now I believe again. Give it a chance and I guarantee you will believe, too.

Kiese Laymon is an award-winning black southern writer, born and raised in Jackson, Mississippi. He is the author of the novel *Long Division* and a collection of essays, *How to Slowly Kill Yourself and Others in America*.

ACKNOWLEDGMENTS

It goes without saying that you never create a book alone. *(H)afrocentric* is the product of many experiences, relationships, and conversations that I've had over the past few years. The journey began in "the town," Oakland, which would be the catalyst to understand a changing neighborhood, at once the home to Black radical leftist movements and the next-door neighbor to a hipster tech invasion. I was trying to understand my own role in this rapidly changing neighborhood and spilled much of it into the pages of this book. I'm grateful to anyone who ever listened to my comic book ideas or read any scripts. Thank you!

I would like to express my most sincere thanks to the following people:

My mother, Nancy Smith, you are the best mother on earth. There isn't one ounce of hyperbole in that statement. Honestly, truly, I couldn't have done this without your love, support, and encouragement my entire life.

My brother, Darren Smith, for your harsh initial feedback and inspiring me with your words of encouragement, mainly your consistent mantra for me to "do better."

My wife and love of my life, Chanda Jones, thank you for being my rock and my emotional support throughout this process.

My bestie, Shelley Oto, your business acumen and marketing expertise has helped me become a better creative. Thank you for picking up the phone in the late hours when I needed you. Don't ever!

My cousin, Yasha Wallin, thank you for lending your editing talents. For free. That's what family is for!

Susie and Steve Lipton, my cousins, thank you for helping me get on my feet when I first moved to New York.

Ronald Nelson, thank you for believing in *(H)afrocentric* from jump. You've grown the comic in ways I could have never imagined. The comic doesn't jump off the page without the synergy of a visionary like you.

Mike Hampton, thank you for contributing your amazing talents to *(H)afrocentric*. We are more colorful for it!

Ras Terms and Robert Trujillo for lending some beautiful art to the backgrounds of *(H)afrocentric*.

Adrian "Age" Scott, thank you for encouraging me from the jump to start a comic book.

Regine Sawyer for being so supportive in bringing the Women in Comics Collective together and introducing me to the future of women creators.

Adrian Arancibia, my mentor and friend, you read over my scripts in their development stages and told me to keep going, thank you.

Dylan Rodriguez, PhD, my ethnic studies professor at UC Riverside, you changed the course of my life and gave me a language to understand the world around me. Thank you for that gift!

And for everyone who has ever read and purchased *(H)afrocentric*, thank you!

Juliana "Jewels" Smith

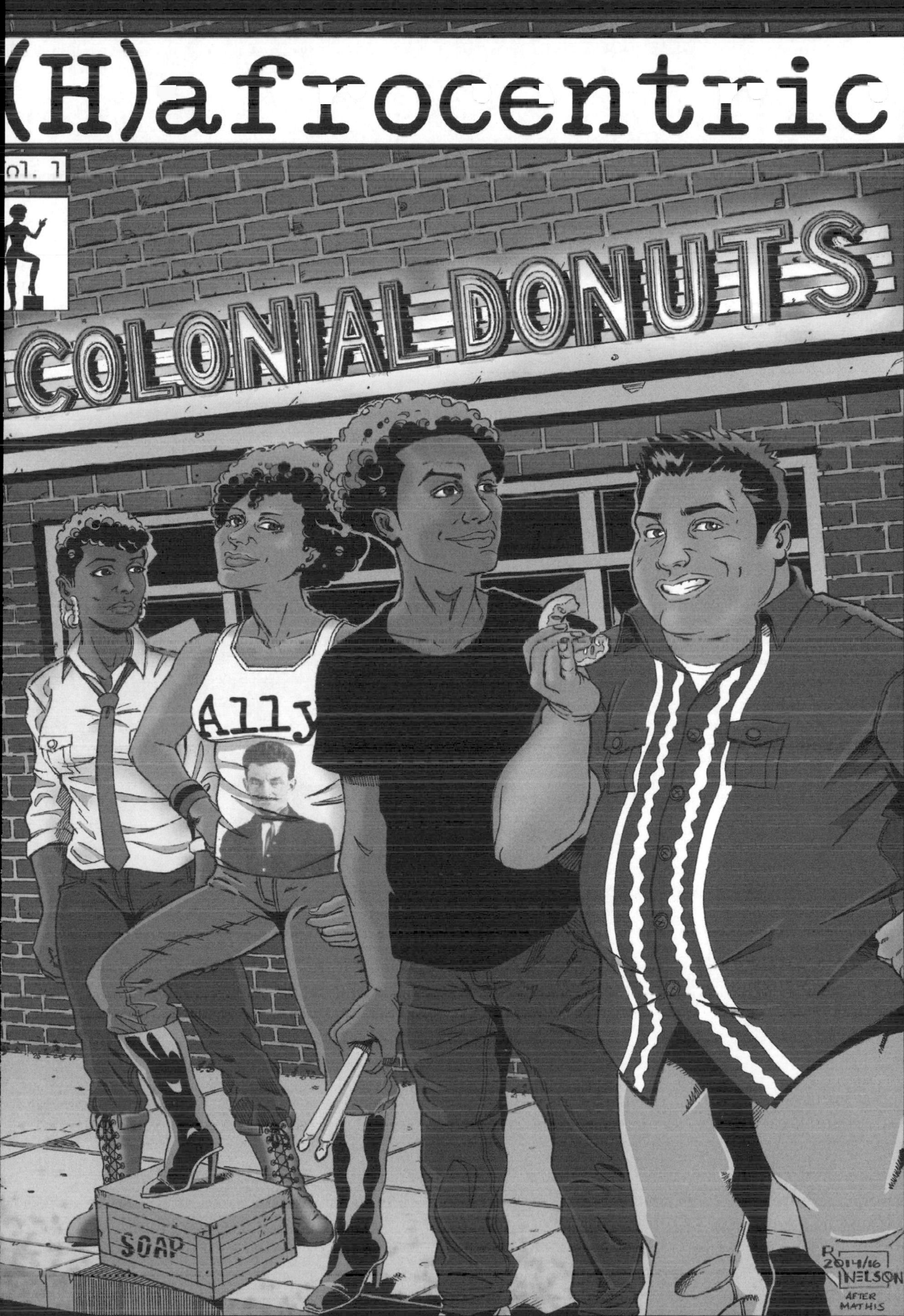

(H)afrocentric
ol. 1
COLONIAL DONUTS
Ally
SOAP
R 2014/16 NELSON
AFTER MATHIS

INTRO.

OAKLAND, CA

POPULATION: 500,000

RONALD REAGAN UNIVERSITY (RRU) IS PERCHED ATOP THE HILLY REDWOODS OF OAKLAND, CA. THIS PRESTIGIOUS UNIVERSITY BOASTS THE LARGEST COMPUTER SCIENCE DEPARTMENT IN THE STATE, SEVEN NOBEL PRIZE FACULTY, AND THE HIGHEST GRADUATION RATES IN THE NATION. WITH STUDENT ENROLLMENT AT 35,000, BLACK STUDENTS MAKE UP LESS THAN 4% OF THE POPULATION, WHILE MEXICAN/CHICANO STUDENTS MAKE UP 10%.

DESPITE THE ACCOLADES RRU PUBLICLY PROFESSES, ITS PRESENCE BIFURCATES THE WORKING CLASS FLATLANDS FROM THE CAMPUS. DURING A CAMPUS BUILDING PROJECT IN 2011, LOCAL TENSIONS AROSE, GALVANIZING IN A COMMUNITY ANTI-GENTRIFICATION MOVEMENT. LIKE MANY US CITIES, OAKLAND HAS BEEN DESTINED FOR THE INFLUX OF GENTRIFICATION'S NEW COFFEE SHOPS, MUTED PRIUS CARS, EXORBITANT RENT, AND HIPSTER APPROPRIATION FOR OVER 20 YEARS.

AT THE NEXUS OF THE SHIFTING DEMOGRAPHICS ARE COLLEGE STUDENTS, AT ONCE PRIVILEGED FOR THEIR UPWARD SOCIAL MOBILITY AND AT ONCE OPPRESSED BECAUSE OF THEIR LITTLE ECONOMIC CLOUT. IT WASN'T UNTIL ONE UNDERGRAD MADE THE CONNECTION BETWEEN THE TWO COMMUNITIES, THAT THE FIGHT AGAINST DISPLACEMENT BURGEONED INTO A CITY WIDE MOVEMENT.

THAT ONE STUDENT IS NAIMA PEPPER–MIDDLE CLASS, BIRACIAL, SUBURBAN-BORN, AND HAILING FROM A TWO PARENT HOME. NAIMA'S PRIVILEGES DON'T DETER HER FROM FIGHTING FOR SOCIAL JUSTICE HOWEVER. HER DISCONTENT AT THE INJUSTICES OF THE WORLD, MERELY EMBOLDEN HER TO CONTINUE THE MOVEMENT

HER COLLEGE STUDENT PROFILE READS:

"RABBLE ROUSER"

"FEMINIST–SO, PROBABLY GAY"

"BLACK NATIONALIST"

"SELF-DESCRIBED HOBBIES: POLITICAL DISSENT"

"SUBJECT SHOULD BE NEUTRALIZED"

PEPPER HAS ASSEMBLED A RELUCTANT BAND OF UNDERGRADUATES INCLUDING HER BEST FRIEND, AND HER BROTHER AND HIS BEST FRIEND, TO LEAD A MOVEMENT. THE CATCH IS, THEY DON'T KNOW IT YET. DISCOVE THE BACKSTORY BEHIND THESE UNDERGRADS AS THEY UNINTENTIONALLY SET OUT TO MAKE HISTORY. WELCOME TO A DAY IN THE LIFE OF (H)AFROCENTRIC.

MILES
THUD!

BOOM! CLAP! BOOM! CLAP!
15 YEARS AGO...
YOU'RE NEVER HERE. AND I DON'T CARE–I'M GOING TO STRAIGHTEN NAIMA'S HAIR! I'M TIRED OF TRYING TO GET THROUGH HER HAIR EVERY MORNING.
.....
THE ART OF WA BY: SUN TZU

KNOCK! KNOCK! KNOCK!
YOU READY TO GO? JUSTICE ISN'T GONNA JUSTIFY ITSELF.
ALLY
BANG!
NAIMA, I'M BUSY.
BUSY?
YEAH.. PLUS, I'M TIRED OF YOU ACTIN' LIKE YOU'RE A MARTYR. YOUR WOKENESS ISN'T GONNA GET YOU A JOB AFTER COLLEGE! TO KEEP IT ONE HUNNIT, I'M TIRED OF BAILING YOU OUT ALL THE TIME.
I'M NOT LEAVING MY ROOM 'TIL I MEET EL ON CAMPUS IN A FEW HOURS–
302
GREAT! I'LL SEE YOU THEN. WEAR COMFORTABLE SHOES.
WHAT?

RENEE

RENEE WAS RAISED TO BELIEVE THAT MEN AND WOMEN EACH HAD A DRESS CODE.
WHAT TO WEAR TODAY?
ANOTHER DAY TO MAKE IT LOOK LIKE I DIDN'T TRY HARD, BUT STILL LOOK GOOD.
"OH, THIS? IT'S A LITTLE SOMETHING I THREW TOGETHER."
"I REALLY LIKE YOUR OUTFIT TOO."
"WHO ME? NOOO...MY HAIR JUST GROWS LIKE THIS."
WHO AM I KIDDING? UGH.

WHAM!
IT DIDN'T OCCUR TO RENEE 'TIL COLLEGE THAT THOSE DRESS CODES WERE MERELY SUGGESTIONS.
HEY! DID I CATCH YOU AT A BAD TIME?
NO, NO...JUST PUTTING MY OUTFIT TOGETHER.
REALLY?
YUP. ALMOST READY.
DO YOU WANT TO BE JANELLE MONAE OR SLEEP WITH HER?
SHE'S MY FASHION ICON!
OK, OK! YOU KNOW, I DON'T CARE EITHER WAY. ARE YOU GOING BACK TO CAMPUS WITH ME? I'M LEADING ANOTHER PROTEST.
YEAH... I'VE GOT TIME.

EL

MIJO, YOU'RE ONLY EATING DONUTS.
"TO BE LOVED AND NOT TO BE ALONE THIS IS OUR CHANCE FOR LOVE, DEAR AND SO COME HEAR, TO ME"**
I KNOW YOU NEED MONEY TO PAY RENT, BUT MY NEXT CHECK DOESN'T COME 'TIL THE BEGINNING OF NEXT SEMESTER. OK?
I WORKED TWO JOBS SO YOU COULD HAVE A BETTER EDUCATION-
I KNOW! AND I'M IN COLLEGE NOW. I'M LIVING THE LIFE YOU DREAMED OF- RIGHT?

WE'RE BEHIND ON RENT AND I CAN'T DO THIS BY MYSELF. YOU HAVE TO GET A JOB.
AND CONTINUE TO TAKE AS MANY CLASSES AS I DO?
THE MANAGEMENT RAISED THE RENT OVER 50% IN THE LAST TWO YEARS. IT'S TOO MUCH–
I'M ALREADY GIVING YOU MONEY FROM MY FINANCIAL AID CHECK. ALRIGHT, ALRIGHT...I'LL GET A JOB!

NAIMA

RONALD REAGAN UNIVERSITY
RONALD REAGAN'S PRESIDENTIAL LEGACY IS BEST KNOWN FOR HELPING TO END THE COLD WAR.
LIES!
AND THROUGH THE GRACIOUSNESS THAT IS THE REAGAN FAMILY, RRU WAS FOUNDED.
LIES!
THE RONALD REAGAN NATIONAL ENDOWMENT SUPPORTS STUDENTS WITH INTERESTS IN PROMOTING DEMOCRACY THROUGHOUT THE WORLD.
LIES! DO NOT LET THEM FOOL YOU. RONALD REAGAN HAD HIS HAND SO FAR UP OTHER COUNTRIES' DEMOCRATIC ELECTIONS, HE WAS PRACTICALLY AN ONCOLOGIST. HIS LEGACY SHOULD REFLECT THE LARGEST MASS INCARCERATION BUILD-UP THE WORLD HAS EVER SEEN!

A11y
LADIES AND GENTLEMEN! WE ARE IN A MOMENT WHERE PEOPLE START TO REWRITE PRESIDENTIAL LEGACIES WITH THE FONDNESS OF A DECEASED PARENT. LET'S NOT FORGET SOME OF THE TERRIBLE THINGS HE ALLOWED TO HAPPEN!
THOSE CHAIRS YOU'RE SITTING ON, THAT FOOD FROM THE CAFETERIA–THEY ARE ALL CONTRACTED THROUGH THE PRISON LABOR OF OUR BROTHERS AND SISTERS–
SOAP
I'LL MEET YOU AT COLONIAL DONUTS IN TWENTY AFTER THEY RELEASE YOU!
A11y

Ally

(H)afrocentric

COLONIAL DONUTS
Cafe
COLONIAL DONUTS
WALK
VIDEO
EL, I'M TRYING TO TELL YOU, OUR ONLY HOPE IS COLONIAL DONUTS...
WHY?
IT'S THE ONLY PLACE THAT WILL SURVIVE THE ONSLAUGHT OF GENTRIFICATION... CAN YOU SAY PO-LICE?
WHAT? IT'S NOT LIKE HE CAN RENT FROM COLONIAL DONUTS, NAIMA!
THINK ABOUT IT... SUGAR AND COLONIALISM EQUAL STABILITY. NO ONE IS GOING ANYWHERE FOR AT LEAST 400 YEARS. *AT LEAST!* THIS PLACE WILL NEVER SHUT DOWN!
EL MAY WANT TO MAKE THIS HIS NEW HOME.
AND?
IF I'M SITTING ON STABILITY AND WEALTH, WOULDN'T SOMEONE RICHER WITH MORE WEAPONS JUST TAKE THE LAND? I MEAN, WE ARE ON **AZTLAN**...
SOAP
ARE YOU SERIOUS, NAIMA?!
SERIOUS! I'M LOOKING FOR ONE OUNCE OF PERMANENCY IN THIS RAPIDLY GENTRIFYNG NEIGHBORHOOD.
NOTHING IS FOREVER, NAIMA.. EVERYTHING CHANGES
NOTHING? HAVE YOU EVER CACHED YOUR **FACEBOOK** ACCOUNT?
HUH? NO?! WHAT DOES THAT HAVE TO DO WITH ANYTHING?
REMEMBER WHEN YOU PISSED ON YOURSELF AFTER YOU RAN THE MILE IN THE 8TH GRADE?
THREE WORDS... **FOR - EV - ER!!**
WHAT? **NAIMA!**

ALL I HAVE TO DO IS SEARCH FOR OLDER POSTS! HAHA!
THE FIRST PLACE YOU SHOULD CONCERN YOURSELF WITH IS THE SUBURBS AND NOT HERE.
EVERYONE KNOWS THE SUBURBS WERE BUILT FOR WHITE FOLKS TO LIVE AS FAR AWAY FROM BLACK FOLKS AS POSSIBLE!
OK, WELL START THERE.
STOP GENTRIFICATION AND ANNOYING JOGGER SUITS IN THE SUBURBS? YOU DON'T UNDERSTAND THE DIFFERENCE BETWEEN BEING PRIVILEGED ENOUGH TO MOVE WHEREVER AND WHENEVER YOU WANT...
...AND BEING PUSHED OUT BECAUSE OF HIGH RENT.
I'M GOING TO START MY OWN ANTI-GENTRIFICATION SOCIAL NETWORKING SITE, FOR BLACK FOLKS, I'LL CALL IT **MYDIASPORA.COM**.
WHENEVER BLACK FOLKS GET TIRED OF WHITE FOLKS THEY CAN JUST UP AND EXODUS TO SOMEWHERE ELSE IN THE VIRTUAL DIASPORA.
AND ANYWAYS, YOU ARE PART WHITE, YOU CAN'T ESCAPE YOURSELF!
PLEASE! I'M ABOUT AS WHITE AS TEENA MARIE'S FIRST ALBUM COVER, MICHAEL MCDONALD'S GOSPEL AD-LIBS AND ROBERT DE NIRO'S TASTE IN WOMEN.
BUT ROBERT DE NIRO LIKES BLACK WOMEN? WOULD THAT MAKE HIM MORE LIKE A BROTHA OR NOT?
Ally
SOAP
Ally

AZTLAN!
HMMM.... MITIERRA.COM?
I MEAN, I THINK ITS ACTUALLY A GOOD IDEA NAIMA!
YEAH, I KNOW IT IS.. MYDIASPORA.COM FUNDED BY THE FORD FOUNDATION AND THE FBI.
NO, IT'S A DUMB IDEA! WHO IS NATIVE TO ANYWHERE ANYMORE?
IN THE WORLD OF MYDIASPORA.COM, WHEN THE ONSLAUGHT OF DOGGY DAY CARE HOTELS IS TOO MUCH, YOU CAN REACH OUT.
Ally
I'D TRY TO GO TO AUSTRALIA FIRST!
YOU'RE GOING TO GET ON MYDIASPORA.COM AND GO TO TO AUSTRALIA? WHY NOT START IN SAY, THE WESTERN HEMISPHERE FIRST?! THE PLACE WHERE HALF OF YOUR ANCESTORS WERE STOLEN AND TAKEN TO..?!
I DON'T KNOW, AUSTRALIA SEEMS REALLY INTERESTING—
INTERESTING? I INTEND MYDIASPORA.COM TO BE A PLACE—
THERE ARE BLACK FOLKS THERE TOO, YA KNOW!
I KNOW THERE'S BLACK FOLKS THERE, EVERYWHERE... IN EUROPE, IN CHINA, HECK WE MIGHT EVEN BE IN ANTARCTICA DOING SOME OF THE SERVICE SECTOR WORK FOR THE DISCOVERY CHANNEL...BUT I DIGRESS.
Discovery CHANNEL
GOT-DAMN! IT'S TOO COLD OUT HERE! I THOUGHT THEY SAID ANASTASIA, NOT ANTARCTICA.
HAD ME BELIEVING I WAS GOING TO DISNEYLAND AND SHIT!

YOU NEED MONEY.
YOU NEED A FUND-RAISER
HMMMPH...
A FUND-RAISER...?
IN ORDER TO GO THROUGH WITH YOUR IDEA, YOU NEED A WEB DESIGNER.
WHAT IF WE DID A SPEAKERS' BUREAU AND HAD ALL MY FAVORITE REVOLUTIONARIES SPEAK? JAMES BALDWIN, GEORGE JACKSON, MALCOLM X, ANGELA DAVIS, NINA SIMONE, JUNE JORDAN, WINNIE MANDELA...
ALLY
OOOH.. OR SUBCOMANDANTE MARCOS, RICARDO FLORES MAGON, GLORIA ANZALDÚA, FRIDA KAHLO, DIEGO RIV—
UGH... WOMANIZER.
NEWSFLASH NAIMA! ALL OF THOSE PEOPLE ARE DEAD!!
REVOLUTIONARIES, THEY'RE REVOLUTIONARIES!
-WHATEVER-
AND THEY ARE NOT ALL DEAD.
MILES HAS A POINT, NAIMA. TRYING TO BRING REVOLUTIONARIES BACK FROM THE DEAD...
MAYBE IRRELEVANT WAS THE WORD I WAS SEARCHING FOR...?
SEEMS LOFTY. ALTHOUGH I'D LOVE TO SEE RICARDO FLORES MAGON.

WELCOME TO MYDIASPORA.COM, THE FIRST AND ONLY ANTI-GENTRIFICATION SOCIAL NETWORKING SITE! MY PEOPLE, ITS GOING TO COME DOWN TO THE ROCK OR THE BULLET. WE CAN'T TURN INTO SAN FRANCISCO OR WILLIAMSBURG! WE MUST STOP GENTRIFICATION AND THE PEOPLE THAT SAY IT'S INEVITABLE! SETTLE YOUR QUARRELS... DO WHAT MUST BE DONE, DISCOVER YOUR HUMANITY AND YOUR LOVE OF REVOLUTION. JOIN US, GIVE UP YOUR LIFE FOR THE PEOPLE!!
IT TAKES A BLACK WOMAN TO RESURRECT MY IDEAS.
Ronald Nelson 2012

HELLO!
ARE YOU THERE?
PHEW... I JUST IMAGINED MYSELF GIVING A SPEECH...
STOP, NAIMA!
I GAVE A MALCOLM X SPEECH, THE PALESTINIAN REMIX, THE ROCK OR THE BULLET. IT WAS ABOUT HOW TO FIGHT STATE VIOLENCE IN THE FORM OF GENTR—
SERIOUSLY NAIMA! STOP!
WE NEED AN IDEA TO HELP FUNDRAISE.
Ally
WHY DON'T YOU HAVE A 90S PARTY? I LOVE THE 90S!
OF COURSE YOU DO, RENEE. YOU'VE KEPT THE BAGGY JEANS AND TIMBOS SINCE FEMALE MCS KEPT THEIR CLOTHES ON.
NO, THE 90S AND 80S PARTIES ARE **OVERDONE.**
WHAT ABOUT THE 50S OR 60S PARTIES? I LOVE SLOW JAMS FROM BACK THEN.
NO, THE BABY BOOMERS GLORIFY THE 60S TOO MUCH AND THE 50S REMINDS ME OF JIM CROW.
OK, WELL THE 30S AND 40S ARE OUT UNLESS YOU WANT TO DRESS UP LIKE A HOBO OR MEXICAN BRACERO...
WHY ARE YOU ALWAYS MAKING GAY JOKES?
I SAID **HOBO**, NOT *HOMO*!
HMMM...IF WE GO BACK ANY FURTHER, WE WILL BE IN SLAVERY AND I'LL HAVE TO DRESS UP IN DRAG.
CAN YOU SAY **NAT TURNER?!**
OMG! SERIOUSLY?

THINK ABOUT ANOTHER FUNDRAISER THEN..
I GOT IT! A BLOCK PARTY FOR LAND, BREAD, AND HOUSING.
TALK ABOUT SOUNDING LIKE THE 60'S AND OLD.
IF PEOPLE STILL DON'T HAVE LAND, BREAD, AND HOUSING, HOW IS THAT OLD?
YOU SHOULD CHECK OUT MY FRIEND JOHN MCDONALD LEE. HE BUILDS WEBSITES.
OKAY, RENEE, WANNA COME WITH?
SURE. I DON'T HAVE CLASS FOR ANOTHER HOUR.

call Mike!

IS THIS THE APARTMENT OF JOHN MCDONALD LEE?
IT'S DARK IN HERE...
HELLO LADIES, WELCOME TO MY SACRED SPACE, WHERE TIME AND PLACE COMBINE.
I NEED TO TWEET A PHOTO OF EVERYONE I MEET, I'M DOCUMENTING MY LIFE, IN REAL TIME.
WTF?!
I WONDER IF HE LIVE TWEETS DURING SEX.
WE ARE LOOKING FOR SOMEONE TO HELP BUILD A WEBSITE.
YOU WERE HIGHLY RECOMMENDED.
EL RAMIREZ...
WHO RECOMMENDED ME?
SHHH... THIS FOOL COULD BE FIVE-O, ALL THIS SURVEILLANCE EVERYWHERE.

I FACEBOOK, SNAPCHAT, AND INSTAGRAM LIVE EVERYONE I MEET. I HAVE A MASTER LIST OF ALL MY INTERACTIONS, RECOMMENDATIONS, ENCOUNTERS.. LIKE A DATA VISUALIZATION OF MY ENTIRE LIFE. IT'S ON MY WEBSITE.
SEEMS LIKE A LOT OF WORK.
ITS CALLED THE BAMBOOZLEDRAGON.COM.. IT COMBINES THE PHILOSOPHIES OF SPIKE LEE AND BRUCE LEE.
HUH?
BRUCE LEE SAID THERE WERE NO LIMITS IN LIFE, JUST PLATEAUS THAT ONE MUST GO BEYOND...
AND SPIKE LEE?
WELL, SPIKE LEE SAID DO THE RIGHT THING, AND THAT'S WHAT I TRY TO DO....
HMMM... MARTIAL ARTS, CONSUMERISM, SPIRITUALITY, AND PHILOSOPHY. INTERESTING MIX.
HAHA! DO YOU KNOW, DO YOU KNOW, DO YOU KNOW...
AND LIKE SPIKE LEE, MY BEST WORK IS THE MOST UNDERRATED.
HA! I HAVE TO TWEET THAT!
CAN YOU HELP US?
WE ARE LOOKING FOR SOMEONE TO BUILD OUR ANTI-GENTRIFICATION SOCIAL NETWORKING WEBSITE, MYDIASPORA.COM.
LET ME CONSULT MY HUMBLE ALTAR DEDICATED TO BRUCE LEE FIRST.

OMMMMMM..... ॐ
BRUCE LEE SAYS SINCE HE'S CHINESE AMERICAN, GREW UP IN OAKLAND, TRAINED KAREEM ABDUL JABAAR, AND–LIKE BLACK PEOPLE–ALL OF HIS ROLES IN AMERICAN CINEMA WERE WRITTEN BY WHITE MEN....
HE SUPPORTS
AND TOLD ME TO DO IT!
GREAT!
THIS BLOCK PARTY HAD BETTER BE GOOD!
IT'LL BE $1,000, WE HAVE A DEAL?
YOU HAVE A DEAL.
A11
WILL YOU HOLD UP THIS SIGN SO I CAN 'TWIT-PIC' YOU?
FLASH!
JOHN McDONALD LEE WORKS FOR ME!!
JOHN McDONALD LEE WORKS FOR ME!!
twitter
faceboo
YouTube
vimeo
GoogLe earth
BY THE WAY, DO YOU KNOW ANYONE THAT HAS SOLAR PANELS?
WE ARE GOING TO USE SOLAR PANELS TO POWER THE BLOCK PARTY.
YES, AS A MATTER OF FACT.
I'M IN MEDITATION CLASS WITH THEM. GO TO 45TH AND MARKET AND ASK FOR AILEEN AND AVERY.
A11

HEY! WELCOME. JOHN SAID YOU WOULD BE COMING PLEASE TAKE OFF YOUR SHOES.
AND CAN YOU TAKE OFF ANY METALS? PERFUME? LIP BALM?
WE JUST WANT TO BE VERY INTENTIONAL ABOUT THE ENERGY FLOWING IN AND OUT OF OUR SPACE.
WE ARE ALLERGIC TO PETROLEUM AND BEESWAX. IF YOU HAVEN'T YET, TRY TOM'S LIP BALM ITS GREAT. IF YOU LIVE NEAR OR ARE CLOSE TO ANY DOGS, PLEASE TAKE OFF YOUR FIRST LAYER OF CLOTHES. THANKS.
HOW'D THEY KNOW I WAS WEARING LIP BALM?
LIKE MY BELT?
YES, PLEASE REMOVE YOUR BELT, SOME PEOPLE ARE ALLERGIC TO METALS.
AND PLEASE REFRAIN FROM USING YOUR CELL PHONES, WE ARE A CANCER AND RADIATION FREE HOUSEHOLD.
WTF?

LUZ, CAN YOU CHIME THE TIBETAN TINGSHA CYMBOLS? FOR SPACE CLEARING...
WE CALL EACH OTHER "LIGHT" IN DIFFERENT LANGUAGES TO AFFIRM THE LIGHT IN ALL OF US...
OH WOW! GREAT!
PLUS *THE SECRET*, HAVE YOU READ IT? IT'S ALL ABOUT POSITIVE INTENTION AS A DAILY PRACTICE.
UGHHH... I CAN'T STAND ***THE SECRET!!***
Ally
HAVE YOU READ *THE SECRET?*
NO. THE ONLY SECRET I KNOW ABOUT IS THE *SECRET GARDEN* WITH BARRY WHITE, AL B SURE, QUINCY JONES, EL DEBARGE, AND JAMES INGRAM—
HUH?
NEVER MIND.
CAN I OFFER YOU SOME KOMBUCHA, GREEN TEA, KALE CHIPS...WE DEHYDRATE THEM OURSELVES.
Ally
WE SELL THEM AT THE FARMER'S MARKET FOR $15 A BAG... BUT FOR YOU, THEY'RE FREE.
UOH... NO THANKS.
OH! I'LL TAKE SOME!
WE HEARD YOU PUT ON SOLAR-POWERED CONCERTS WITH BIKES.
YES, WE DO. BUT WOW, YOUR TONE WAS REALLY HARSH. LUMIERE CAN YOU RING THE CYMBOLS AGAIN?

WOULD YOU BE WILLING TO DONATE YOUR SOLAR PANELS?
IT'S THE *LEAST* YOU CAN DO...
WELL, WE CAN... WE JUST ASK THAT YOU PRACTICE INTENTIONAL-HEALING-SPIRITUAL-ENERGY PRACTICES WITH YOUR CONCERT.
WTF?!...DOES THAT MEAN?
Ally
WHAT'S YOUR CONCERT FOR? AND WHO IS PLAYING?
IT'S A BLOCK PARTY TO RAISE MONEY FOR A WEBSITE WE ARE BUILDING, MYDIASPORA.COM.
OH, I LOVE AFRICA. BEEN THERE A FEW TIMES... KENYA IS WONDERFUL. I REALLY DISCOVERED MY TRUE SELF THERE.
UGH!
WE ARE GONNA HAVE THE ROOTS, DEAD PREZ, CHANCE THE RAPPER, CHILDISH GAMBINO, KEHLANI–
OH! I LOVE DEAD PREZ!!
OH! I LOVE PAUL MOONEY TOO!
WHY IS SHE LYING? WE CAN'T AFFORD *THEM*!
OF COURSE YOU DO.. FIRST PAUL MOONEY THEN DEAD PREZ.. WHAT'S NEXT?
LOOKS LIKE WE GOT A DEAL. SEE YOU AT THE BLOCK PARTY.
YES, AFTER WE GET THE SOLAR PANELS.

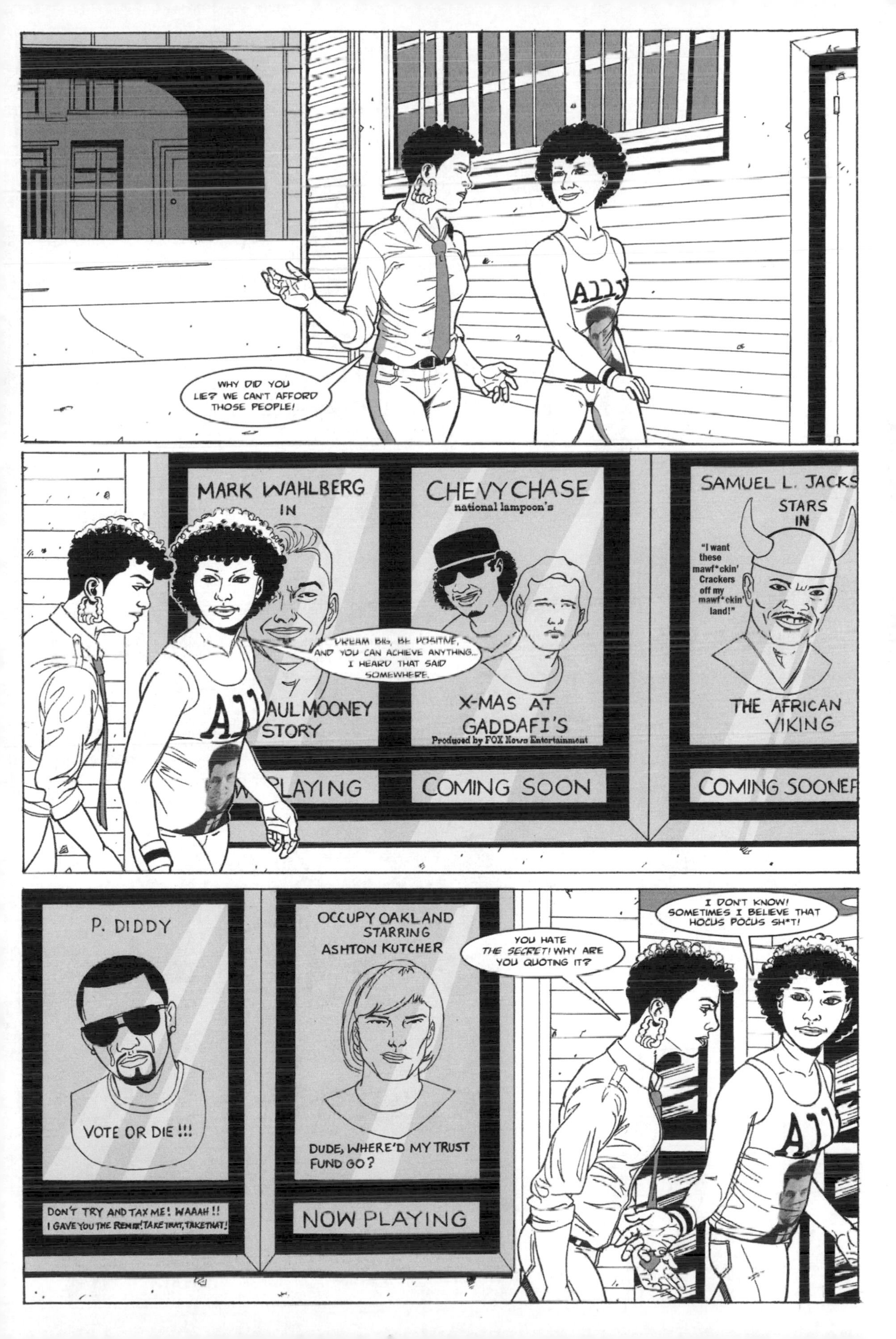
WHY DID YOU LIE? WE CAN'T AFFORD THOSE PEOPLE!
MARK WAHLBERG IN
AUL MOONEY STORY
CHEVY CHASE
national lampoon's
X-MAS AT GADDAFI'S
Produced by FOX News Entertainment
SAMUEL L. JACKS
STARS IN
"I want these mawf*ckin' Crackers off my mawf*ckin' land!"
THE AFRICAN VIKING
PLAYING
COMING SOON
COMING SOONER
DREAM BIG, BE POSITIVE, AND YOU CAN ACHIEVE ANYTHING... I HEARD THAT SAID SOMEWHERE.
P. DIDDY
VOTE OR DIE !!!
DON'T TRY AND TAX ME! WAAAH !!
I GAVE YOU THE REMIX! TAKE THAT, TAKE THAT!
OCCUPY OAKLAND STARRING ASHTON KUTCHER
DUDE, WHERE'D MY TRUST FUND GO?
NOW PLAYING
YOU HATE THE SECRET! WHY ARE YOU QUOTING IT?
I DON'T KNOW! SOMETIMES I BELIEVE THAT HOCUS POCUS SH*T!

SAMMY SOSA
School of Beaut
Starting Salary for Oakland Police & Teache Positions are at $80K
GEORGE JACKSON ENDOW CHAIR IN AFRICAN AMERICA STUDIES AT UC BERKELEY
BUSH AND CHENEY TRIED AS WAR C
JVC
AND BESIDES, I'VE NEVER SEEN YOU BE PLEASANT AROUND WHITE FOLKS WITH DREADLOCKS...
I KNOW, IT DOES MAKE ME UNCOMFORTABLE. LIKE PUBLIC RESTROOMS AND MY VISION OF THE COMING APOCALYPSE...
AJ
EBONY
CONDI AND COLIN SUBJECTED TO TRIBUNAL FOR CRIMES AGAINST HUMANITY!!!!
VOGUE
ASSATA SHAKUR...
NEW JERSEY'S NE GOVERNOR!!!

San Jose Mercury N
NELL ON THE PHONE AT PELICAN BAY
UGO PINELL FREE AFTER 40 YRS
NEMPLOYMENT HITS 20%
Incoming freshman class at Ronald Reagan University Black population 1.5% for the 22nd year in a row since Prop. 209.
GOING OUT OF BUSINESS
Everett and Jones BARBEQUE
Star
JUDGE CLARENCE THOMAS: SERVING TIME IN SHU AT PELICAN BAY!
Whole Foods now as affordable as Grocery Outlet!

JOHN IS GONNA BUILD THE WEBSITE, WE GOT SOLAR PANELS FROM "LIGHTS" TO RUN THE BLOCK PARTY.
NOW, WE JUST NEED THE BLOCK AND TO RECRUIT SOME TALENT.
SO, HOW'D IT GO?
THIS IS STILL A DUMB-ASS IDEA!!
NO. ITS NOT! IT'LL BE THE FIRST TIME IN HISTORY THAT THOSE BEING AFFECTED BY GENTRIFICATION CAN VIRTUALLY REDIRECT THEIR NEW NEIGHBORS AND PLACE THEMSELVES WHERE THEY CHOOSE. GOTTA START SOMEWHERE.
LIKE I SAID. DUMB IDEA. YOU CAN'T STOP GENTRIFICATION ONLINE.
YOU'RE SO INEBRIATED WITH THINKING THINGS WILL NEVER CHANGE THAT YOU NEVER EXPERIMENT. YOU'RE A ROBOT!
I DON'T EVEN KNOW WHAT THAT WORD MEANS! BUT THIS IS A ROBOT THAT CAN PLAY THE DRUMS.
WHY DON'T YOU PLAY THE DRUMS AT THE BLOCK PARTY?
THAT'S THE ONLY THING I'LL DO!
AHA! SO YOU'RE IN?
I GUESS I AM.
Ally

WHERE ARE WE GOING TO HAVE A BLOCK PARTY?
HEY Y'ALL WE GOT THAT GOOD GREEN TEA, CARDAMOM, LEMON BALM WITH SPEARMINT, ROOIBOS...WE GOT THAT!
YOU ARE SELLING TEA ON CAMPUS?
YUP-YUP, WE GOT THAT... TEA GAME SWAG!
TEA? WTF? YOU DON'T HAVE ANY TAMPICO, SODAS, RED-BULL, JUICE...?
NO. TIMES ARE TOUGH. WE DIDN'T GET OUR FINANCIAL AID CHECKS.
PROBABLY THE GHOST OF RONALD REAGAN'S PAST. HE MAKES IT HARD ON THE 3.9% OF US ON CAMPUS.
WE STARTED SELLING TEA. WE KNOW WHERE WE ARE. MIX CDS, DVDS, R.I.P. T-SHIRTS FOR MAC DRE AND MICHAEL JACKSON WEREN'T GONNA CUT IT.
WE ON THAT GOOD TEA HUSTLE. WE CALL IT MIX-TEA.
WELL, GOOD LUCK TO Y'ALL...
YOU DON'T WANT YOUR CHAKRAS OPEN SIS? IT'S ALL MADE FROM PH BALANCED, ALKALINE WATER.
GREEN TEA, HONEYBUSH, AYURVEDIC SWAG!!

ALKALINE WATER SWAG!
WTF!?
CAN'T. TOO BROKE. IT'S TOO HARD NOT TO SMOKE OUR OWN TREES.
TELL YOUR FRIENDS WHEN THEY EAT TOO MANY CHILI CHEESE FRITOS OR BURRITOS LATE AT NIGHT FROM THE TACO TRUCK... WE GOT THEM, FOR REAL.
...AND HAVE YOU EVER BEEN BROKE AND LOOKED FOR FOOD IN YOUR FRIDGE?
WHY DON'T YOU JUST SELL TREES IN THE DORMS LIKE EVERYONE ELSE?
NO SUCH THING AS BROKE SWAG. OXYMORON! CREATIVE SWAG ONLY!!
GOT YOU. THAT'S A GOOD LOOK THEN.
SO, YOU WANT SOME GREEN TEA? IT'LL HELP YOU FOCUS ON YOUR SCHOOL WORK.
BRUH, DOES IT LOOK LIKE I DO ANY WORK IN SCHOOL?
LOOK, WE NEED YOUR ADVICE. WE ARE THROWING A BLOCK PARTY.
OH, YOU WANT MY ADVICE BUT YOU DON'T WANT TO BE HEALTHY?
LET ME GET SOME GEN-MA-CHAI, AND SOME CARDAMOM TEA.
THAT'S A GOOD LOOK, SIS. YOU HAVE INDIGESTION PROBLEMS?
NO!
CARDAMOM ALSO RELIEVES FLATULENCE, JUST IN CASE, SIS I'M LOOKIN' OUT.
A11
SOAP

WE ARE TRYING TO HAVE A BLOCK PARTY, ANY SUGGESTIONS ON WHERE WE SHOULD HAVE IT?
A BLOCK PARTY? I AM THE BLOCK, SIS.
BLOCK PARTY SWAG!
WE WANT IT TO BE "DIVERSE." NEEDLESS TO SAY, WE CAN'T HAVE IT ON RONALD REAGAN U CAMPUS.
I'VE LIVED DOWN THE BLOCK FROM RRU CAMPUS MY WHOLE LIFE. IT DOESN'T LOOK THE SAME AS IT DID WHEN I WAS GROWING UP, BUT IT'S STILL THE BLOCK.
BEFORE...
STAR VI
AFTER...
STAR VI
HELLO... 911....
YES, MY NEIGHBORS ARE DISTURBING THE PEACE.
SENDING A CAR OUT NOW.. WE WILL BE THERE IN 3 MINUTES STAT!"
IS IT EASY TO BLOCK IT OFF?
CONSIDER IT DONE. I RUN THE BLOCK. WHAT DAY DO YOU NEED IT?
WE HOLD DOWN THE BLOCK, SWAG!!
THAT EASY, HUH?
Ally

WE WOULD DO IT OCTOBER 8TH.
I DON'T KNOW, SIS. THAT IS THE SAME DAY AS THE ALL MELANISTIC PEOPLE'S FESTIVAL.
WHAT IS THAT?
OH, YOU DON'T KNOW BROTHA? IT'S A FESTIVAL TO LET THE PEOPLE KNOW WHO THE TRUE GODS AND THE TRUE EARTH ARE...
...AND OF COURSE WHO THE REAL ENEMY IS....
WHO IS THE SAID ENEMY?
DAMN, SIS. IF I HAVE TO TELL YOU THAT, THEN IT DEFEATS THE PURPOSE.
WE DON'T WANT TO COMPETE WITH THE ALL MELANISTIC PEOPLE'S FESTIVAL, BUT THAT IS THE BEST DAY FOR US TO DO IT.
I'LL MAKE IT HAPPEN FOR YOU. LIKE I SAID, I DON'T REPRESENT THE BLOCK, I AM THE BLOCK.
AND AS "THE BLOCK," YOU CAN SHUT IT DOWN FOR US?
Ally
YES.
YOU ARE LIKE THE *WU-TANG CLAN* OF ORGANIZING. YOU CAN ORGANIZE THE WHOLE BLOCK.
Ally

HOW MANY MEMBERS OF THE WU-TANG CLAN ARE THERE?
OH, YOU DIDN'T KNOW? I WAS SUPPOSED TO BE THE 10TH MEMBER OF WU-TANG CLAN.
WHAT HAPPENED?
I WAS ONLY 2 WHEN WU-TANG'S FIRST ALBUM CAME OUT AND I WAS BORN AND RAISED ON THE WEST COAST. BUT AT THE TENDER AGE OF 8, I MASTERED QI GONG, SHAOLIN KUNG FU, AND THE BREATHING TECHNIQUES OF INEDIA OR BREATHARIANISM AS IT'S KNOWN IN THE WEST.
WOW, IMPRESSIVE.
THIS N*GGA HAS GOT TO BE KIDDING!?
SO WHAT BROUGHT YOU TO RRU?
I HAD TO APPEASE MY MOM. AS A GOD AND A STUDENT OF SUPREME MATHEMATICS I KNOW THAT I WAS BROUGHT HERE TO SPREAD KNOWLEDGE.
80 DEGREES WHEN I TELL THAT TRICK PLEASE...
HOW MANY LETTERS ARE IN RONALD REAGAN'S NAME? HIS FULL NAME?
RONALD WILSON REAGAN... 6-6-6....
I REST MY CASE. KNOWLEDGE, WISDOM, AND UNDERSTANDING...
ASIATIC BLACKMAN, SWAG!
SO, SEE YOU OCTOBER 8TH?
YUP-YUP....
SEE YOU THEN.
Ally
TO BE CONTINUED...

WHEN YOU BUY THIS BOOK, YOU SAVE A STARVING AFRICAN. AMERICAN.
Ally
SOAP

(H)afrocentric
Vol. 3
Ally
SOAP
R 2013 NELSON
MY DIASPORA.COM PRESENTS:
THE BLOCK ADE PARTY

Ally

RING
RING
RIIING!
(GASP)!
Ally
HEY, NAIMA!
OH... HEY!
DID I WAKE YOU?
IT'S OK. I JUST HAD A DREAM I WAS RUNNING FROM THE COPS...WITH MY HEELS ON? I'M NOT SURE WHY.
THEY SAY RUNNING IN YOUR DREAMS SIGNIFIES ANXIETY, NAIMA.
THEY ALSO SAY REVOLUTIONARIES CAN'T WEAR HEELS. HMMPH...

WWW.MyDiaspora.com
WORLD ATLAS
I JUST SENT OVER THE MOCK UPS FOR MYDIASPORA.COM.
MYDIASPORA.COM THE 1ST AND ONLY SOCIAL NETWORKING SITE DEDICATED TO ANTI-GENTRIFICATION IS ALMOST READY TO GO ONLINE.
GREAT. I'LL HAVE A LOOK.
I DECIDED TO GO WITH PETER'S PROJECTION MAP OF THE WORLD INSTEAD OF THE MERCATOR MAP OF THE WORLD.
I KNEW THERE WAS A REASON WHY I ENDED UP WORKING WITH YOU.
AND DON'T FORGET TO TWEET ABOUT ME!
I WON'T.
FINALLY, THE DAY HAS COME. THE ONE PLACE IN THE WORLD THAT IS FREE OF GENTRIFICATION. THE VIRTUAL WORLD! AND AFRICA IS IN THE MIDDLE. HOW APROPOS!
NOW, FOR WORLD DOMINATION! AHA...AHAHA.... AHAHAHAHAHAHA!!!
JUST KIDDING. THIS ISN'T A CAPITALIST COMIC! THAT IS UNLESS YOU'VE JUST BOUGHT THIS...HAHA! NO PROMO.

STOP BROKE ON BROKE CRIME!
THE PEOPLE THAT LIVE HERE ARE BEING DISPLACED
OCTOBER 5TH
SUP, SISTAS. SUP, BRUH.
HEY, WE NEVER CAUGHT YOUR NAMES.
I'M KWAME BUT YOU CAN CALL ME... TRUE JUSTICE OR TJ FOR SHORT.
(WTF?! RAPPERS DON'T EVEN CHANGE THEIR NAMES ANYMORE? KANYE WEST, DRAKE, J. COLE, DANA OWENS...? WHAT IS UP WITH NAMES LIKE TRUE JUSTICE? MORE LIKE "FREE DUMB.")
AND I'M RAHSAAN, BUT YOU CAN CALL ME FREEDOM OVER BITCHES... OR FOB FOR SHORT.
I'M GOING TO START RENAMING MYSELF WITH ANITA BAKER'S DISCOGRAPHY...SWEET LOVE. BODY AND SOUL. SAME OL' LOVE. THIS IS RIDICULOUS!
NAME CHANGE GAME, SWAG!
HMMMM...
BYE-BYE-BYE-BYE-I-I-I-I-I BYE-BUUUUUY... HAVING A CAREER THAT SPANS AS LONG AS SADE'S AND TAKES THE SAME AMOUNT OF R&R BREAKS, DOES HAVE ITS PERKS.
lly

SO THIS IS THE SPOT. WHAT DO YOU THINK?
CAN WE DO THIS WITHOUT THE POLICE?
WHERE AM I GONNA PLAY?
PLEASE, FAM, CALM DOWN.
MY THIRD EYE VISION IS GONNA HAVE THIS PLACE LOOKIN LIKE...
ENTER THE DRAGON
POPULATION: HELLA WU TANG
HELLA KILLA BEES
HELLA KILLA ARMY MEMBERS
HELLA SUNS OF MAN
EXIT: BABYLON
HOME. *OUR* HOME. OR WHERE WE SHOULD BE...

HEY, EL...
SUP, Y'ALL.
CITY OF OAKLAND
RESIDENT HAS LESS THAN ONE WEEK TO FIX BLIGHTED HOUSE.
OTHERWISE, HOUSE WILL BE FORECLOSED ON.
YOU DON'T LOOK SO GOOD.
JUST STRESSIN' OVER THIS EVICTION.
LOOKS LIKE YOUR NEIGHBOR HAS IT PRETTY BAD, TOO.
YEAH, SHE'S AN ELDERLY WOMAN WHO HAS OWNED THAT HOUSE FOR OVER 30 YEARS. SHE HAS A WEEK TO FIX UP HER PLACE BEFORE THEY EVICT HER.
THEY...?
THE PO-LICE, RENEE.

LOOK. WE NEED TO SHUT DOWN THE STREET FOR THE BLOCK PARTY.
WHY ARE YOU EVEN DOING THIS, NAIMA? FOR ME? FOR MY FAMILY? IT'S NOT GOING TO HELP. THIS IS AZTLAN! AND IT'S BEING CONQUERED, AGAIN!
I'M...I MEAN...WE ARE DOING THIS FOR YOU AND--
YOU ARE DOING THIS FOR YOU, NAIMA!
WE NEED TO MAKE SURE THE BLOCK PARTY DOESN'T GET SHUT DOWN AND WE NEED TO RAISE THIS MONEY FOR MYDIASPORA.COM!
NAIMA, DON'T WORRY ABOUT MY MOM AND ME. WE'LL BE FINE.WORRY ABOUT MRS. WILDERSON WHO'S BOUT TO BE KICKED OUT OF HER PLACE!
WHO??
SHE'S THE LADY THAT SELLS ROSETTA STONES.
HMM...WE SHOULD TALK TO HER.

Rosetta Stone
Learn To Speak English Spanish French Arab Hier Wu-
Rosetta Stone
Love Language with an intro by Talib Kweli
Rosetta Stone
The King's English: Yes, Negro open this up to get a job
Rosetta Stone
Translate 50 Cent & Common's mumbled interview speech.
Rosetta Stone
I'm scared of Black People And did I mention I have a small penis?
Geraldo Rivera
WILDERSONS BOOKS
HOW Y'ALL DOING?
I'M GLAD TO SEE YOUNG FOLKS OUT HERE DOING SOMETHING POSITIVE. LORD KNOWS THESE HOODLUMS AND GANGBANGERS OUT HERE ARE UP TO NO GOOD. I TOLD 'EM THEY SHOULD HAVE MORE POLICE HERE.
WELL...THANK YOU, I GUESS...MRS. WILDERSON HOW LONG HAVE YOU BEEN LIVING HERE?
I'D SAY IT'S BEEN OVER 30 YEARS.
WHEN DID YOU GET THE EVICTION NOTICE?
TWO WEEKS AGO.... TOLD ME I HAD LESS THAN A MONTH TO FIX UP MY HOUSE OR WELLS FARGO IS GONNA COME IN AND TAKE MY HOUSE. THIS WHOLE THING IS MAKING ME SICK. I'M JUST NOT TRYIN' TO NOT CATCH *THE SUGAR!*
THE *SUGAR?*
DIABETES.
MRS. WILDERSON, WE ARE ATTEMPTING TO DO WHAT NO COMMUNITY HAS SUCCESSFULLY DONE... STOP GENTRIFICATION.
WELL LORD KNOWS I NEED SOME GENTLEMEN IN MY LIFE.
HUH?
NO, MRS. WILDERSON... WE WANT YOU TO BE ABLE TO STAY IN YOUR HOME ON YOUR FIXED INCOME. AND MAKE SURE THE BANK DOESN'T COME AND TAKE YOUR HOUSE.
AWW... BAAY-BEE,YOU'RE SO SWEET. I STILL SELL MY BOOKS AND I PUT MY FAITH IN GOD.
THEN, MRS. WILDERSON THIS BLOCK PARTY IS FOR YOU.
WELL THANK YA, BABY.

THIS IS A DUMB IDEA. YOU ARE NOT JOHN Q AND THIS IS NOT AVATAR.
I'M NOT LISTENING TO YOU. NOW, TO THE TASK OF SETTING UP THIS BLOCK PARTY.
YO, SIS...THERE'S A COUPLE OF WAYS TO TRY AND PREVENT THE BLOCK PARTY FROM GETTING' SHUT DOWN.
ME AND SOME HOMIES CAN DO SECURITY. OUR WING CHUN TECHNIQUES ARE ALMOST PERFECTED. AND I'D LOVE TO TRY THAT SHI*T OUT ON SOME MAWF------
DO WE NEED TO GET PERMITS?
NAH, WE HAVE TO BE MORE STRATEGIC THAN THAT.
WE DON'T NEED NO STINKIN' PERMITS. HA!
LOOK. THERE'S ONLY TWO WAYS THE BLOCK GETS SHUT DOWN. SOMEONE IS MURDERED, THERE'S A PARADE OR, THE POLICE QUARANTINE US LIKE THE MOVE ORGANIZATION LIVES HERE.
THAT WAS THREE, BRUH....

THAT LAST SCENARIO IS OUT OF THE QUESTION. WE NEED SOMETHING ELSE.
ONALD REAGA UNIVERSITY LIBRARY
WHY DON'T WE STAGE A HIP HOP PROCESSION, THE DEATH AND REBIRTH OF TUPAC?
LIKE HOW LATINOS WALK THROUGH THE STREETS AND PRETEND JESUS JUST GOT KILLED, ONLY OURS WILL BE FOR 2PAC. HA!
2 PAC DIES
LO SIENTO, TÍA.
NO, THAT WONT WORK. PLUS, THE TUPAC HOLOGRAM STOLE ALL THE TUPAC RESURRECTION SHINE.
WE NEED A MORE SECURE PLAN THAN THAT.

Tyler Perry's Black Family Values Starring Pregnancy Jones and the Bible
Tyler Perry Jannes Version
A film by the poor... Groundhog Day
Hello debt... again
WE NEED TO FUNDRAISE FOR MYDIASPORA.COM!
TRUE.
AND WE NEED TO SHUT DOWN THE BLOCK IN ORDER TO HAVE A BLOCK PARTY.
TRUE.
AND WE NEED MUSICAL TALENT.
TRUE.
SO, I SAY...
BLOCK OFF THE STREET...THEN WE CHARGE $75 TO PEOPLE WHO HAVE LIVED IN THE NEIGHBORHOOD LESS THAN 2 YEARS, $55 FOR 5 YEARS $10 FOR 10 YEARS, BEEN HERE LONGER THAN 20 YEARS, GET IN FREE. WE ASSEMBLE THE BEST BAND THAT EVER EXISTED. GET THEM TO PLAY FOR FREE BY GIVING THEM ALL--
SOAP
STOP! NO COSIGN. DUMB ASS IDEA! AND, RENEE, WHY DO YOU SOUND LIKE A 90'S BAD-BOY HIP-HOP BACKGROUND VOCAL?
HOW DO YOU EVEN PLAN ON GETTING THESE ARTISTS?
"TREEEEEEWWW...UHHH... UHHH...WHA-WHAT? YA GOT IT GOIN ON... WHA-WHA-WHAT?"

HENRY LOUIS GATES: "HOW I SURVIVED A POLICE ENCOUNTER AND HOW YOU CAN TOO!"
BROWN PAPER-BAG SPEAKER SERIES MITT ROMNEY: "GREEN LIVING.. AND I DO NOT MEAN PUBLIC TRANSPORTATION
DRAKE: "FROM THE SUBURBS TO THE STREETS; YOU GOTTA HAVE CHUTZPAH!" MEG WHITMAN: ON AFFIRMATIVE ACTION
ONE, THEY'LL DO IT BECAUSE IT'S A GOOD CAUSE.
WHAT'S THE CAUSE? THEY'RE ALL RICH NOW. THEY DON'T NEED TO PLAY FOR CHARITY! BESIDES THE ONLY CHARITY I KNOW IS THIS GIRL I USED TO GO TO SCHOOL WITH, SHE HANGS OUT ON 53RD AND SAN PABLO......
........SHE'S OUT THERE AT NIGHT TRYING TO GET PICKED UP, BUT SHE READS NOVELS WHILE SHE'S ON THE STREET... CRAZY.
HENRY LOUIS GATES: "HOW I SURVIVED A POLICE ENCOUNTER AND HOW YOU CAN TOO!"
BROWN PAPER-BAG SPEAKER SERIES MITT ROMNEY: "GREEN LIVING.. AND I DO NOT MEAN PUBLIC TRANSPORTATION
ISN'T THAT RUDY HUXTABLE IN "MADEA GOES TO JAIL"?
DRAKE: "FROM THE SUBURBS TO THE STREETS; YOU GOTTA HAVE CHUTZPAH!" MEG WHITMAN: ON AFFIRMATIVE ACTION
OH, WHOOPS. I GUESS I GOT REAL LIFE MIXED UP WITH A TYLER PERRY FILM. HIS FILMS ARE SO REAL.
THEY'LL DO IT BECAUSE IT'S GOING TO BE FILMED LIVE ACROSS THE WORLD ON MYDIASPORA.COM

ALLS I'M SAYIN' IS THE STAGE HAS GOTTA FACE MECCA, THE HOLY LAND. WE HAVE TO PRAY AND STAY TO THE EAST...
MECCA? N***A WHAT ARE YOU TALKING ABOUT?
SIS. I GOT YOU. IT'LL BE HANDLED.
AND BRUH, YOU NEED TO READ MORE. THEY TRY TO CONFUSE YOU WITH POLITRIX AND OTHER DELUSIONS LIKE SPACE TRAVEL.
BUT WE BEEN TRAVELING WITHOUT NASA FOR YEARS.
WHAT??
AND WHY HAVEN'T THEY BEEN BACK TO THE MOON, HUH?
I'M SAYIN'... IF IT'S THAT CLOSE, WHY NOT GO AGAIN? I MEAN I CAN SEE IT FROM HERE.
THEY DIDN'T GO! AND NOW THEY TRYIN' TO GIVE US DISEASES LIKE AIDS.
WHERE WHITE BLOOD CELLS ATTACK THE MELANISTIC CELLS...
...THAT S**T IS RACIST!
IS THIS N***A SERIOUSLY SERIOUS?
YOU NEED TO READ, HOMIE!
A NI**A PARABLE! HASH TAG THAT!
"AIDS IS RACIST" BY: RECOGNIZE X

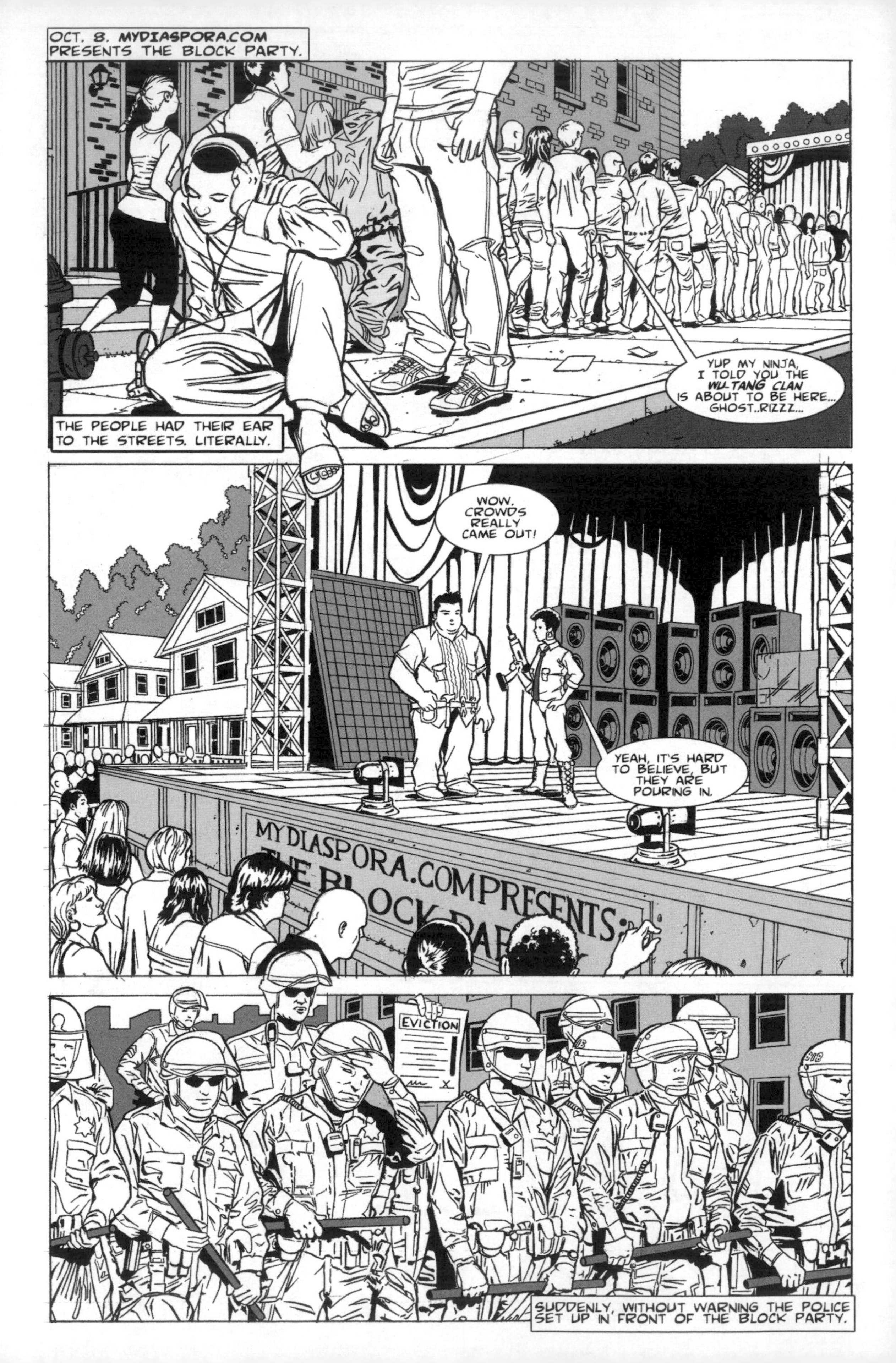
OCT. 8. MYDIASPORA.COM PRESENTS THE BLOCK PARTY.
YUP MY NINJA, I TOLD YOU THE WU-TANG CLAN IS ABOUT TO BE HERE... GHOST..RIZZZ...
THE PEOPLE HAD THEIR EAR TO THE STREETS. LITERALLY.
WOW. CROWDS REALLY CAME OUT!
YEAH, IT'S HARD TO BELIEVE, BUT THEY ARE POURING IN.
MYDIASPORA.COM PRESENTS:
EVICTION
SUDDENLY, WITHOUT WARNING THE POLICE SET UP IN FRONT OF THE BLOCK PARTY.

Arab Spring USA
POLICE
I CANT BELIEVE THEY CAME IN WITHOUT WARNING. THEY DIDN'T EVEN STOP TO READ US OUR RIGHTS. THIS IS WHAT DEMOCRACY LOOKS LIKE!! THIS IS WHAT DEMOCRACY LOOKS LIKE!!
FREE TIBETAN WHALES
WHAT IN THE WORLD? THIS LOOKS LIKE THE NEGRO OLYMPICS.

ALL MELANISTIC PEOPLE'S FESTIVAL
YOU GUYS ARE THE REPS FOR THE ALL MELANISTIC PEOPLES... I THOUGHT--?
I'M MORE CONFUSED THAN LAURYN HILL'S OUTFITS AND MUSIC TEMPOS.
DIDN'T HEAR YOU GUYS COME IN.
I GUESS THE PURR OF YOUR ELECTRIC CAR MADE IT IMPOSSIBLE TO DETECT YOUR WHEREABOUTS.
YES... YES WE ARE.
THAT'S RIGHT. WE HAVE ALWAYS BEEN IN ALIGNMENT WITH AMPP.
BUT I THOUGHT YOU HAD TO BE... YA KNOW?
IT'S A NEW DAY. EVERYONE IS MIXED. THE CORNERSTONE OF JUSTICE IS THAT EVERYONE BE TREATED EQUALLY AND EVERYONE SHOULD BE ABLE TO ENTER INTO ANY ORGANIZATION OR INSTITUTION THEY SEE FIT. THAT'S THE AMERICAN DREAM.

WE JUST APPRECIATE EVERYONE'S CULTURE.
I MEAN, I'M IRISH AND ITALIAN....AND BESIDES, AT THE END OF THE DAY, WE ARE ALL AFRICAN AND COME FROM AFRICA.
WE DON'T HAVE TIME TO DISCUSS YOUR WET DREAMS OF ANTHROPOLOGY. THE POLICE ARE HERE. DID YOU GUYS MANAGE TO GET THE SOLAR PANELS?
YES...
THEY ARE IN THE PRIUS.
GOOD, WE WILL NEED THOSE TO START.
HURRY AND PUT THEM UP SO WE CAN GET ON THE MIC BEFORE THE COPS MAKE THEIR WAY UP HERE.

HEY! NAIMA JUST SAID THE COPS ARE HERE! I THOUGHT YOU SAID THERE WOULD BE NO POLICE!
WELL, WE SET UP A DECOY.
WHAT DECOY?
I CALLED THE ALL MELANISTIC PEOPLES PARTY AND TOLD THEM THEY SHOULD SHUT DOWN COLONIAL DONUTS, THE ONLY DONUT SHOP OPEN 24 HOURS FOR 50 MILES...
...EVERY COP IN TOWN SHOULD HAVE BEEN THERE TO STOP THE POTENTIAL SHUT DOWN.
LOOK! THIS BLOCK PARTY IS NOW A BLOCKADE PARTY! WE NEED YOU TO–
PUSH BUTTON FOR DRIVEWAY WALK SIGNAL
BAP!
BOP!
POW!
THUD!
PONG!
PING!
POP!
WAP!
THUD!

AHEM. IS THIS THING ON...? YES, HELLO...CAN YOU HEAR ME? POLICE ARE THE 99.9% TOO. WE ALL HAVE RIGHTS! DON'T LET THEM TAKE MRS. WILDERSON'S HOUSE! WE MUST OCCUPY!
MYDIAS
COMPRESENTS:
ADE
PARTY

YOUR METAPHORS ARE... FAMILIAR.
I DROP LYRICS LIKE STOOL SAMPLES: UNSANITARY.. YOUR RHYMES ARE LIKE HALLMARK: STATIONARY.
I'M MARRIED TO THE STRUGGLE, BRAD AND ANGELINA... I'M FROM THE BAY, SO I SUPPLEMENT MY DIET WITH SPIRULINA.
YOUR METAPHORS ARE... FAMILIAR.
YOUR METAPHORS ARE... FAMILIAR!!
YO...
POLICE GOT NO LOVE FOR US, YOU KNOW THAT: ZERO... WHEN THEY COME AFTER ME.. I DODGE 'EM LIKE WHITE GIRLS: ROB DE NIRO.
WHEN I KICK THESE RHYMES I'M IN RARE FORM: YOGA POSES.. GOT YOU OPEN OFF MY SWAG: HYP-NOSES.
YOUR METAPHORS ARE... FAMILIAR!!
YOUR METAPHORS ARE... FAMILIAR!!

RUN THAT BACK DJ!!
(PHEW)
I DON'T EAT PORK, I DON'T EAT PORK... AND NEITHER SHOULD YOU... MESS AROUND AND CATCH DIABETES, TYPE TWO.
THAT NO GOOD FILTHY PIG...
THAT SCHEMING, HONKING, NOSE TALKING.. FILTHY SWINE.... NO FRIEND OF MINE.
SO GET OUTTA BABYLON.. EAT VEGGIES AND PRACTICE RAMADAN.
FAST IF YOU NEED TO, NOW THAT'S WEALTH.
BECAUSE WHAT? THE PORK...
AIN'T NO GOOD FOR YOUR HEALTH. BIAAAAACH!!

!!!
SWIPE
THIS BLOCK PARTY IS FOR MYDIASPORA.COM, THE FIRST AND ONLY PLACE ON EARTH FREE OF GENTRIFICATION! AND THIS IS ALSO FOR MRS. WILDERSON!
CLAP CLAP
CLAP CLAP
WE SET OUT TO MAKE THIS NEIGHBORHOOD AFFORDABLE FOR THE PEOPLE THAT HAVE BEEN LIVING HERE FOR DECADES. AND WE HAVE MADE PROGRESS. NOT ENOUGH. BUT WE HAVE MADE SOME. THANK YOU FOR BELIEVING IN THE IDEA OF MYDIASPORA.COM!
WOO-HOO!!
CLAP CLAP
CLAP CLAP
CLAP CLAP CLAP
TO HEAR THE REST OF THE BLOCK PARTY, SCAN THIS CODE!
VISIT SOUNDCLOUD.COM/HAFROCENTRIC

OH SH*T! WHAT HAPPENED TO MRS. WILDERSON?
OH NO! THEY KILLED HER!
NO, WHITE SUPREMACY KILLED HER... KILLED GERONIMO PRATT... MICHAEL JACKSON... WHITNEY HOUSTON... KILLED ALICIA KEYS' CORNROWS...
NAIMA! STOP. IT'S PROBABLY THESE SMELLY ASS DOGS AND THAT STENCH THAT KILLED HER. DAMN! THESE FOOLS STINK!
LOOKS LIKE WE WON THE BATTLE, BUT LOST THE WAR AGAINST GENTRIFICATION.
NAIMA, THIS WAS ALL YOUR IDEA. NOW LOOK WHAT'S HAPPENED.
I DIDN'T CREATE THIS MESS!
BUT YOU MADE IT WORSE!!

NAIMA, AT LEAST YOU TRIED TO DO SOMETHING.
WHAT'S THE POINT? I TRY TO BE LIKE MY HEROES AND I FAIL.
EVERYONE GREAT FAILS. MALCOLM X WENT TO PRISION FOR YEARS BEFORE HE BECAME A GREAT LEADER. RICK ROSS HAS LOTS OF HITS, BUT HE'LL PROBABLY DIE OF HYPERTENSION AND DIABETES BEFORE THIS COMIC BOOK ENDS. AND GUCCI MANE TATTOOED AN ICE CREAM CONE ON HIS FACE. FAILURES.
I KNOW YOU ARE TRYING TO MAKE ME FEEL BETTER MILES. I JUST CANT HELP BUT THINK IF I DIDN'T DO THE BLOCK PARTY, MRS. WILDERSON WOULD STILL BE ALIVE.
WAIT!! I KNOW WHAT WE CAN DO!!!
Ally
SOAP
WILDERSON'S LIBRARY
Branch of the People
STAY TUNED FOR VOL. 4!

DRAW YOUR IDEAL PLACE TO LIVE.

TAKE A PHOTO. SEND IT TO NAIMA @HAFROCENTRIC ON TWITTER, FACEBOOK, OR INSTAGRAM. NAIMA WILL CHOOSE THE MOST INNOVATIVE DRAWING TO WIN A (H)AFROCENTRIC GIFT BAG!

COLORING FUN!

COLOR IN ALL THE TOOLS THAT YOU NEED TO START A MOVEMENT!

SELF CARE

A REVOLUTIONARY SPIRIT

DISGUISE

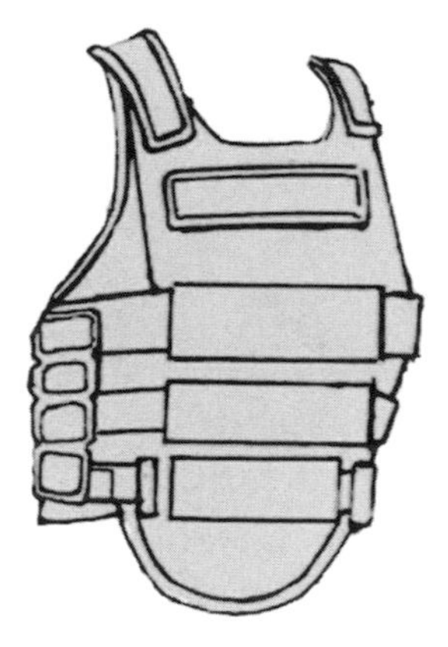

PROTECTION

VOLUME CONTROL

THE MOVEMENT ALWAYS NEEDS PEOPLE. LET US KNOW IF WE FORGOT ANY TOOLS! @HAFROCENTRIC

WHAT'S A SUPERHERO TO A REVOLUTIONARY?

(H)afrocentric

HAFROCENTRIC.COM

(H)afrocentric
ol. 1
COLONIAL DONUTS
Ally
SOAP
R 2014/16 NELSON
AFTER MATHIS

(H)afrocentric

Ally

(H)afrocentric
Vol. 3
Ally
SOAP
R. 2013 NELSON
MY DIASPORA.COM PRESENTS:
THE BLOCK ADE PARTY

(H)afrocentric

HAFROCENTRIC.COM

(H)afrocentric
Vol. 4
WILL WORK FOR THE REVOLUTION
SOAP
WINNER 2016
BEST WRITER
2015 NELSON

(H)afrocentric
R 2015 NELSON
HAFROCENTRIC.COM

(H)afrocentric
Vol. 4
WILL WORK FOR THE REVOLUTION
A11
MOD
SOAP
WINNER 2016
glyph COMICS AWARDS
BEST WRITER
2015 NELSON

Will Work For the Revolution

With the help of a fairy godmother, Naima Pepper is able to land a senior internship as a RACIAL TRANSLATOR. But will she be able to get through the internship without being fired for her fiery soapbox moments?

Copyright © 2016 (H)afrocentric
www.hafrocentric.com

HANDS OFF
ASSATA!
FREE
ALL MY HEROES ARE REVOLUTIONARIES. ALL MY HEROES ARE DEAD. HOW CAN I BE LIKE THEM AND GET A JOB...? HMMM...WHAT WOULD GEORGE JACKSON DO?
Ally
毛主席语录
THE WRETCHED OF THE EARTH
FIRE NEXT TIME
A MODEL FOR LIBERATION
Angela Davis -Autobiography
YOU KNOW I'D NEVER LIVE A MOMENT ON MY KNEES!
POOF!
YOU KNOW WHAT YOU NEED TO DO THEN--
I KNOW, BUT I NEED AN INTERNSHIP AND THE FIRST ONE I HAVE CAN'T BE A REVOLUTIONARY ONE. I HAVE TO BUILD UP TO THAT.
WHAT? WHAT DO I NEED TO DO? TELL ME!!
ATA!
ALL
YOU KNOW...
POOF!
UGH. I READ ANGELA DAVIS TOO EARLY IN MY LIFE... SIGH.

I THOUGHT YOUR DREAMS WERE SUPPOSED TO GIVE YOU ANSWERS, NOT MORE QUESTIONS.
'BRRRRRRRING'
HEY. WHAT'S UP?
HEY.
WHAT'S UP WITH YOU? STILL WORKING ON FINDING A SENIOR INTERNSHIP?
BEEN LOOKING ON CRAIGSLIST. EVER NOTICE THAT IT'S OVER-WHELMING AND HAS MORE OPTIONS THAN THE DEMOCRATIC PRIMARY, YET NONE OF THEM ARE GOOD? THERE ARE LOTS OF INTERNSHIPS AS A CAMPAIGN ORGANIZER OR REGISTERING PEOPLE TO VOTE.
THE ONES THAT TRY TO GET YOU TO SIGN PETITIONS?
LIKE SAVING THE WHALES AND SEA TURTLES. MEANWHILE, I CANT SAVE ENOUGH MONEY TO BUY--
WELL, GOOD LUCK WITH THAT!
YOU ALREADY GOT AN INTERNSHIP?
AT HOT TOPIC. I'M A STUDENT CONSULTANT FOR THE GENDER-BENDING DEPARTMENT. THEY WANT TO REACH THE LGBT COMMUNITY AND UNDERSTAND THE PHENOMENON OF SKINNY JEANS.
THAT'S EASY. THE ANSWER TO THAT LIES IN WHY THEY SOLD OUT OF THEIR TONGUE RINGS IN THE 90S.

ARE THERE ANY JOBS FOR REVOLUTIONARIES?!
YOU ARE NOT A REVOLUTIONARY! GET AN INTERNSHIP OR FOLLOW YOUR PASSION.
JUST BECAUSE YOU'VE BEEN GIVEN THE GIFT OF BEING MUSICALLY INCLINED FROM BIRTH--
AND STUNNINGLY HANDSOME!
I GUESS THERE IS NO SUCH THING AS A REVOLUTIONARY INTERNSHIP. BUT THINGS MUST BE BAD IF I CAN'T GIVE AWAY MY LABOR.
LOOKS LIKE I'LL BE GRADUATING BEFORE YOU! HA! I'M GOING TO BE SANDING THE DRUMSTICKS AT QUESTLOVE'S SCHOOL OF DRUMMING.

BACK ON RONALD REAGAN U CAMPUS.
GOT MY INTERNSHIP LINED UP!
QUESTLOVE'S SCHOOL OF DRUMMING
DON LEMON'S Recruiting for a CNN internship in S.A.M.B.O.
[Stop All the Madness by Blaming Others]
LOOKING FOR BLOG WRITERS!
**MUST HAVE AUTHENTIC STORY OF GROWING UP IN THE STREETS (OR STUDIED SOMEONE WHO HAS GROWN UP IN THE STREETS. OR SEEN A MOVIE ABOUT SOMEONE GROWING UP IN THE STREETS.)
I DIDN'T KNOW THEY HAD INTERNSHIPS FOR MEXICANS WHO DRESS LIKE THEY'RE FROM CUBA.
WHILE YOU'RE OVER HERE HATIN' ON PEOPLE'S DREAMS, I'M GETTING AN INTERNSHIP IN REAL ESTATE.
BOUT TO TAKE THE LAND BACK! FOR AZTLAN!
I'M A RECRUITER FOR THE HIEROGLYPHICS SUMMER CAMP. WE TAKE BROTHAS AND SISTAS WHO HAVE NO KNOWLEDGE OF THEMSELVES, AND FIX THEIR COLONIAL MENTALITY. LIKE AN AFRO-CENTRIC BOOTCAMP.
SHHH... CANT SAY NOTHING, AIGHT.
THAT'S RIGHT.

THIS IS SO FRUSTRATING! WHERE DO ALL THE RESUMES AND COVER LETTERS OF PEOPLE WHO DON'T GET JOBS GO...?
Ally
HELLO NAIMA. I'M YA FAIRY GODMOTHER. I ALSO BEAR A STRIKING RESEMBLANCE TO FANNIE LOU HAMER.
WILL WORK FOR THE REVOLUTION.
POOF!
WOOOOW!! WHAT SHOULD I CALL YOU?
THEY CALLLLL MEEEEEEEEEE... THE RECYCLER, A NEW AGE FAIRY, THE ECO FAIRY OR THE E-FAIRY, EVEN A HIPPIE, BUT NEVER A HIPSTER. MY OUTFIT MAY BE SKINTIGHT BUT I DON'T HAVE A TRUST FUND! AND I DON'T RIDE BIKES! OBVIOUSLY, I JUST TRANSPORTED HERE.
WILL WORK FOR THE REVOLUTION.
WELL, I GUESS I DO HAVE SOMETHING IN COMMON WITH HIPS-TERS. I LIKE TO PARACHUTE INTO "UNKNOWN" LANDS AND SAY THINGS LIKE "TRAVELING HERE IS REALLY DANGEROUS." "HELLUVA FLIGHT" OR "GREAT MEXICAN FOOD, BUT I WOULDN'T LIVE HERE."
OH?
LET ME GIVE YA A LESSON YA WON'T GET IN SCHOOL.

WELCOME! I'VE WON THE GREENEST FAIRY AWARD IN 2011 AND 2015. I'VE RECEIVED EVERY FAILED RESUME AND COVER LETTER SUBMISSION ON THE PLANET. I'VE BUILT MY HOME ON THE DISAPPEARING HOPES OF A SALARIED AND SUSTAINABLE LIFE. I MADE MY CURRENT HOUSE OUT OF THOSE PAPERS. STACKS ON STACKS ON STACKS!
MOST EFFICIENT
MOST BLUNT FAIRY
THE REALIST FAIRY
NINA SIMONE AWARD: MOST MISUNDERSTOOD
Most Likely To Have My Chapter In History Replaced By Martin Luther King
I THOUGHT THOSE DREAMS OF A SALARIED LIFE DISAPPEARED DURING THE REIGN OF RONALD REAGAN. I DIDN'T KNOW THAT DREAMS AND HOPES HELD WEIGHT.
OF COURSE THEY DO. HAVE YOU MEASURED HOW FAR HOPE CAN GO...?
I RELUCTANTLY VOTED FOR OBAMA. SO, I GUESS, ALL THE WAY TO THE WHITE HOUSE?
THE CIVIL RIGHTS MOVEMENT HAD DREAMS OF A MORE JUST WORLD AND--
NOW THERE ARE MORE BLACK PEOPLE IN PRISON TODAY THAN THERE WERE SLAVES IN THE 19TH CENTURY AND DURING SOUTH AFRICAN APARTHEID--
I SAID THEY HELD WEIGHT! I DIDN'T SAY WHAT KIND. I'M HERE TO ANSWER SOME OF YOUR MOST BURNING QUESTIONS AND GIVE YA TWO WISHES.
A WISH? TO ME? ONLY IN A COMIC BOOK.

SINCE YOU'VE ANSWERED THE QUESTION OF WHERE ALL THE RESUMES GO, I DO HAVE A WISH. I WISH FOR A SENIOR INTERNSHIP WHERE I CAN MAKE LOTS OF MONEY & NOT WORK FOR SOMEONE RICH. PREFERABLY, I'D BE BUILDING TOWARDS THE REVOLUTION
I SAY REPARATIONS NOW REPARATIONS TOMORROW REPARATIONS FOREVER!
I SAID A WISH! NOT AN ALTERNATE UNIVERSE WHERE COLUMBUS NEVER SET FOOT IN THE AMERICAS AND AFRICANS DIDN'T BECOME ONTOLOGICALLY NONEXISTENT!
HUH??
I CAN ONLY MAKE DREAMS COME TRUE IN THE REALITY THAT WE LIVE NOW, LOVE. I CAN'T FIX WESTERN CIVILIZATION.
NO MAKING BLACK LIFE MATTER?
NOW YA GETTIN' THE PICTURE.
FAIRY. HOW ABOUT A PAID INTERNSHIP THAT'S INTERESTING AND IS ABLE TO BUILD ON MY SKILLS?
YA CAN WORK IN THE SERVICE SECTOR OR THE PUBLIC SECTOR.
WHICH ONE YA WANT?
SECOND CHOICE.
POOF!

FAIRY GIVES NAIMA AN INTERNSHIP AS A **RACIAL INTERPRETER**. SHE TRANSLATES THE BEHAVIOR, GESTURES, ACTIONS AND MOST OF ALL, THE LOUD SILENCE BETWEEN THE RACES. SMALLER DEPARTMENTS DEDICATED TO CLASS, GENDER, AND SEXUALITY; REMAIN IN THEIR INFANCY STAGES.
HELLO NAIMA!! WELCOME TO THE DIVERSITY INTERPRETATION CENTER FOR KINDNESS, WELL-BEING, AND DEVELOPMENT OR DICK WAD. I'M AILEEN AS YOU KNOW. WE KNEW YOU WOULD BE A GREAT FIT FOR OUR **RACIAL APTITUDE PROGRAM** *OR* **RAP**. WE ARE SO HAPPY TO HAVE YOU ON BOARD AS A RACIAL INTERPRETER!
THANK YOU FOR HIRING ME.
RACE
CLASS
GENDER
BLACK TWITTER
BLACK TUMBLR
THE MAJORITY OF OUR INTERPRETING COMES FROM WHITE PEOPLE WHO REALLY WANT TO UNDERSTAND BLACK PEOPLE. THEY ARE CONCERNED WITH THE LANGUAGE BEING USED AND HOW TO INTERPRET CERTAIN PHYSICAL MOVEMENTS. YOU KNOW--THE INTRICACIES OF COMMUNICATION.
SOMETIMES WE GET IT THE OTHER WAY AROUND. BLACK PEOPLE WANT TO UNDERSTAND WHITE PEOPLE. THEN THERE'S CROSSOVER BETWEEN THE RACES, MEXICANS WANT TO UNDERSTAND ASIANS AND ASIANS WANT TO UNDERSTAND WHITES, ETC.
UH HUH. I SEE.

AFTER THE RESISTANCE MOVEMENTS OF 2014, THE FEDERAL GOVERNMENT IMPLEMENTED THE DIVERSITY INTERPRETATION CENTER FOR KINDNESS, WELL-BEING, AND DEVELOPMENT (DICK WAD) IN ORDER TO MEND THE "RACIAL TENSION & RIOTS."
WE NEED YOUR EXPERTISE IN RAP, THE TRANSLATION OF BLACK PEOPLE TO WHITE PEOPLE. YOU WILL BE EXPLAINING TO WHITE PEOPLE THE ACTIONS AND/OR BEHAVIOR OF BLACK PEOPLE. AND SINCE YOU ARE MIXED--
ALMOST ALL BLACK PEOPLE CAN DO THIS JOB. BLACK FOLKS KNOW WHITE FOLKS BETTER THAN THEY KNOW THEM--
I'M SORRY?
JUST SAYING.
WELL, WE ARE JUST GOING TO HAVE YOU WORKING ON THAT TRANSLATION SINCE THAT IS WHAT OUR FEDERAL GRANT FUNDS.
I CAN DO THE OTHER WAY AROUND TOO.
THAT WON'T BE NECESSARY. JUST TELL US ABOUT "YOUR PEOPLE" FOR NOW.

THIS FEELS LIKE THE TIME I WAS SO BROKE I RESPONDED TO A CRAIGSLIST AD AND I TRIED TO SURGICALLY GIVE MY EGGS AWAY. THEY TOLD ME I WASN'T "THE RIGHT FIT."
Ally
RONALD REAGAN UNIVERSITY IS GREAT, HUH? GREAT EDUCATION, BEAUTIFUL CAMPUS, KNOWN FOR ITS ACTIVISM, AND AMAZING REDWOODS.
I GUESS...
WE ARE GOING TO PUT YOU OUT IN THE FIELD AND I'LL BE HERE WATCHING. NO BIG DEAL. KIND OF LIKE TRAINING DAY BUT I AM DENZEL AND YOU ARE...WELL, YA KNOW.
RULES OF ENGAGEMENT
1. RECOGNIZE THAT TIME & SPACE CHANGE MEANING.
2. ALWAYS MAINTAIN NUANCES & AMBIGUITIES.
3. NOT EVERYTHING CAN BE TRANSLATED.
THIS IS THE BEST YOU CAN DO MISS FAIRY?

DICK WAD IS SET UP TO READ MULTIPLE SCREENS AND SITUATIONS. ONE AT A TIME, NAIMA AND AILEEN GO THROUGH CUSTOMERS' PRESSING QUESTIONS CONCERNING RACE. AILEEN OFFERS HER WISDOM AFTER INTERNING FOR 5 YEARS AT DICK WAD AND EARNING A B.A. IN ANTHROPOLOGY.
WE JUST RECEIVED A CALL FROM-- MRS. MCCARTHY. LOOKS LIKE HER HAND JUST GOT SLAPPED AWAY BY A BLACK WOMAN BEEEEEE-CAAAUUSE SHE TOUCHED HERRRR HAAAAIR...HMMM..
THIS IS EASY.
I'M SO GLAD YOU ARE HERE TO HELP! WHY DO SO MANY BLACK WOMEN HATE THEIR NATURAL HAIR? I'D LOVE TO HAVE IT! AND YOUR HAIR IS WONDERFUL TOO BY THE WAY!
WHAT THIS BLACK WOMAN IS TRYING TO TELL YOU IS STOP PETTING ME LIKE I AM A ZOO AND YOU ARE PUSHING ME TO RECALL THE HISTORICAL TRAUMA OF MY ANCESTORS BY EITHER:
A) REMINDING ME OF THE WORLD FAIRS STARTING AT THE END OF THE 19TH CENTURY, WHERE PEOPLE WHO LOOKED LIKE ME WERE PUT ON DISPLAY TO REMIND WHITE CIVIL SOCIETY OF THEIR OWN ADVANCEMENTS AND ACCOMPLISHMENTS
OR....
B) REMINDING ME OF SLAVERY. WHEN ANY WHITE PERSON IN THE U.S. OF A HAD UNWAVERING ACCESS TO BLACK PEOPLE'S BODIES. ANYTHING FROM TOUCHING TO SEXUAL ASSAULT WAS PERMISSIBLE AND SIMPLY A PART OF BEING A WHITE--
WHOA! NAIMA, THAT WAS INFORMATIVE, YET, HOW SHOULD I SAY THIS? WORDY AND CONDESCENDING. IT'S NOT WHAT YOU SAY, BUT HOW YOU SAY IT. TRY A LIL MORE NBA PLAYER POST-GAME INTERVIEW. CONCISE, WITH SUBTLE REFERENCES TO TEAMWORK OR STAFF WORK ETHIC. A LITTLE LESS CORNEL WEST. CAN YOU DO THAT?
THANKS FOR THE FEEDBACK AILEEN.

THIS IS FROM ANNIE IN PITTSBURGH.
WHY DON'T BLACK PEOPLE LIKE OPRAH?
WHY DO WHITE PEOPLE LOVE OPRAH?
HUH?
EXACTLY.
SILENCE ENSUES.
NAIMA. I LOVE THE SOCRATIC METHOD TOO, BUT THAT MAY NOT BE OUR BEST BET HERE. WE REALLY WANT TO MAKE OUR CUSTOMERS FEEL AT EASE. LET'S TRY ANOTHER ONE FROM–

WHY DON'T BLACK PEOPLE TAKE RESPONSIBILITY FOR THEIR ACTIONS?
CAN YOU BE MORE SPECIFIC?
WHY DO THEY ALWAYS BLAME THE COPS FOR GETTING KILLED WHEN THEY KILL THEMSELVES ALL THE TIME?
...AT THE SAME TIME!
Ally
YOU KNOW SOMETIMES METAPHORS ARE THE BEST WAY TO GET YOUR POINT ACROSS. THEY RESONATE WITH PEOPLE, GIVES THEM SOMETHING TO GO HOME AND THINK ABOUT.
AND THEY FEEL SAFER?
PLEASE HAND ME A GLASS OF ALCOHOL AND MATCHES AS I ATTEMPT TO SPIT FIRE OUT OF MY MOUTH AND START THE REVOLUTION...
EXACTLY! I KNOW HOW IT IS. I USED TO BE AN ACTIVIST ON MY COLLEGE CAMPUS. I HAVE FAMILY MEMBERS THAT ARE BLACK AND NEPHEWS THAT ARE HALF MEXICAN. IT'S REALLY IMPORTANT THAT YOU LET PEOPLE COME TO THEIR OWN CONCLUSIONS. YOU CAN DO IT NAIMA.
SOAP
SOAP

TO BOOST MORALE, AILEEN HAS NAIMA TRANSLATE WHITE PEOPLE TO BLACK PEOPLE.
WHY DON'T WHITE PEOPLE JUST HAVE THEIR OWN COUNTRY AND STOP KILLING US?!
THEY DO. ZIMBABWE, CONGO, SOUTH AFRICA, THE PHILIPPINES, THE HOOD---
OKAAAAY! ON SECOND THOUGHT, LETS GO BACK TO THE OTHER TRANSLATION.
SLAVERY WAS SO LONG AGO, WHY DO---
AHHHHHHHHH!!!!!!!!!! STOP. THIS MIGHT BE THE WORST JOB IN THE WORLD!
NAIMA! THAT IS IT. I REALLY THOUGHT YOU WOULD BE GREAT AT RACIALLY TRANSLATING BUT I'M GOING TO HAVE TO ASK YOU TO LEAVE.
BLACK ANGER MANAGEMENT
WRITTEN: REV. AL SHARPTON
INTRODUCTION BY: UNION OF BLACK POLICE OFFICERS
BROOKLYN AGAINST
Misogynoir Is Not A Cinematic Style
Written & Directed By Ava DuVernay
PLEASE, AILEEN NO! I'M NOT GOOD AT SUGAR COATING.
STRATEGY AND MESSAGING ARE MORE IMPORTANT THAN TRUTH, NAIMA. USING THE RIGHT LANGUAGE IS REALLY IMPORTANT TO CONSIDER WHEN YOU DO THIS JOB OR ANY OTHER JOB. SORRY TO SAY BUT THE ONLY THING YOU WILL BE SUGARCOATING IS THE GLAZE AT COLONIAL DONUTS.
*SCAN THE CODE OR GO TO: HTTP://GOO.GL/WFXIJJ
I UNDERSTAND. I'LL FOCUS ON MY METAPHORS AND ALIEN SCIENCE FICTION. I'LL RE-READ ANIMAL FARM. PLEASE DON'T FIRE ME! I WON'T BE ABLE TO GRADUATE WITHOUT THIS INTERNSHIP.
YOU CAN EITHER START GIVING TEXTBOOK ANSWERS TO RACIAL INTERPRETING AND APOLOGIZE TO OUR CLIENTS, OR YOU CAN LEAVE HERE WITHOUT A TERMINATION RECORD. YOUR CHOICE.

DO I HAVE A FAIRY GODMOTHER OR A WICKED STEPMOTHER?
EXSCUUUUUUSE ME?
WILL WORK 4 SOME. JUSTICE. SOME. WHERE. SOME. TIME
POOF!
OUCH! MISS FAIRY. I DIDN'T KNOW YOU WERE THERE.
YA DIDN'T NOTICE ME HUH? F**K YA MEAN YA DIDN'T NOTICE ME? I LOOK LIKE TWO SCOOPS OF CHOCOLATE ICE CREAM HANGING OVER A WAFFLE CONE!
I MEANT I'M GLAD YOU'RE HERE. (SIGH) MISS FAIRY, WHY DID YOU DO THIS TO ME? I AM NOT A RACIAL INTERPRETER. I'M--
DO YA THINK IT'S EASY TO BE THIS SIZE AND FIT INTO THESE TIGHT-ASS TIGHTS?! HUH? HUH?
WELL, NO I GUESS?
NO ONE EVER SAID YOU'RE A RACIAL INTERPRETER. THAT WOULD PUT YA IN-A EXISTENTIAL CRISIS. NAIMA, YA DOING THE WORK OF A RACIAL INTERPRETER, BUT YOU'RE NOT SIMPLY THAT.
I KNOW BUT-
IF YOU WANT TO BE A REVOLUTIONARY SO BAD, IMAGNE WHAT THAT LOOKS LIKE. IS IT JUST ONE THING?
WILL WORK 4 SOME. JUSTICE. SOME. WHERE. SOME. TIME.
NO. NO AMERIE.

LET ME ASK YA SOMETHING. WHAT IS THAT?
A SOAPBOX.
SOA
YA STOP SEEING WHAT YOU THINK YA KNOW. YOUR INTERNSHIP, YOUR SOAPBOX, ALL HAVE INFINITE POSSIBILITIES! THAT ISN'T JUST A SOAPBOX--
YOU GOT ME F***ED UP. -AFRICAN AMERICAN PROVERB
Ally
BUT MISS FAIRY I--
STOP THINKING YA KNOW EVERY-GOTDAMN-THING!
YOU GOT ME F***ED UP. -AFRICAN AMERICAN PROVERB
THINK LIKE A CHILD!!
THINK LIKE A CHILD. THINK LIKE A CHILD. WHAT DOES A CHILD THINK...?
HUNGRY! VEGAN MILK. TIRED. BRIGHT. HUGS. HUNGRY!

NEXT DAY...
HOW ARE YOU?
I'M NOT GOING TO BE ABLE TO GRADUATE. UNLESS, I SELL MY SOUL.
IF IT MAKES YOU FEEL ANY BETTER, I WAS WORKING IN THE DEPARTMENT OF GENDER BENDING AT HOT TOPIC AND THEY WERE TELLING US TO 'REALLY PUSH THE ENVELOPE WITH FASHION.'
I DECIDED TO SWITCH ALL OF THE MEN'S CLOTHING LABELS WITH THE WOMEN'S CLOTHING...SAME FOR THE SHOES.
AND?
I GOT FIRED. I ALWAYS WANTED THE MEN'S SHOES SECTION TO SAY WOMEN'S SHOES SO MY PARENTS WOULD BUY THEM FOR ME WITHOUT ASKING ME WHY I WANT TO DRESS LIKE A BOY.
RENEE. MOVE TO THE EAST COAST. NO ONE WILL EVER NOTICE YOUR BAGGY JEANS, SLIGHT BULGES, AND TIMBERLAND BOOTS, IT'S TOO COLD.

NAIMA AND RENEE MAKE THEIR WAY BACK TO RRU.
WHAT YOU NEED TO DO, SIS, IS JOIN THE SQUAD.
WE GOT ACROBATICS FOR YOUR MENTAL AND PHYSICAL.
WHERE DID YOU ALL COME FROM...?
NAIMA, I'VE NEVER SEEN YOU GIVE UP. EVER.
THEY CALL IT BURNOUT AND I CAN'T GO ON.
THERE COMES A TIME IN EVERYONE'S LIFE WHEN THEY HAVE TO DO LIKE A CHILD AND--
GODDAMN!!
DO YOU LISTEN TO...
ANYTHING I SAY?!

WHO ARE YOU?!
HOW'D WE JUST GET BEAT UP BY A LITTLE PERSON?
MY EYE. MY EYE. I CAN'T SEE!
I AIN'T LITTLE! I'M YA ANCESTOR!
I Sing (and Scream) Cuz I'm FREE!
IS THAT YOUR COUSIN NAIMA?
MISS. ALLOW ME TO INTRODUCE MYSELF. I TEACH HIEROGLYPHICS, PYRAMID BUILDING, AND ALL THE ANCIENT TEACHINGS OF EGYPT. I MEAN KEMET. IT'S REAL LIFE SKILLS THAT CAN HELP SAVE OUR PEOPLE. BECAUSE THE BLACK MA—
I Sing (and Scream) Cuz I'm FREE!
F*CK ARE YOU TALKING AB--
MISS. MISS. I'MA LET YOU FINISH. BUT ANCIENT EGYPT HAD ONE OF THE GREATEST CIVILIZATIONS OF ALL TIME! YOU DO KNOW ABOUT KEMET, DON'T YOU?

FAIRY CHANNELS THE ANCESTORS TO GIVE A TALK TO THE YOUNG SENIORS OF RONALD REAGAN UNIVERSITY.
IF I'VE LEARNED ANYTHING IN MY LIFE AND AFTERLIFE, IT'S THAT YOU ONLY GET A FEW CHANCES TO BE FREE.
Would Nat Turner Do?
MISS, WE NEED TO GET BACK TO OUR ROOTS. SELF-DETERMINATION, KNOWLEDGE OF SELF, KEMETIC SPIRITUALITY--
What Would Nat Turner Do?
YA EITHER DIE FIGHTING TO GET FREE OR YA SIT AND CRITIQUE THE PEOPLE GETTIN' FREE!

I-I-I-I CAN'T GET INTO TROUBLE... I HAVE TO FINISH AN INTERNSHIP.
YOU WERE FIRED FOR GIVING WOMEN MORE ANKLE SUPPORT. YOU HAVE NOTHING TO LOSE RENEE!
THEY CAN'T STEAL OUR VOICES!
WE SHOULD START A COUP! RIGHT FAIRY?
WOOSH!
LIKE TAKING OUT A LATIN AMERICAN PRESIDENT? I'M WITH IT!
EVERY ACT OF RESILIENCY, IS AN ACT OF LOVE. EVERY ACT OF JUSTICE, IS AN ACT OF LOVE. EVERY ACT TO DIGNIFY BLACK LIFE, IS AN ACT OF LOVE. ......
ACT ACCORDINGLY!

BREAK ON 3! 1-2-3!
BREAK!
*TO HEAR WHAT WAS SAID IN THE HUDDLE, SCAN THE CODE...OR GO TO: WWW.SOUNDCLOUD.COM/HAFROCENTRIC
DICK WAD HEADQUARTERS.
SLAM!
BANG!

EXIT
Ally
LADIES AND GENTLEMEN! WE'RE TAKING OVER!
WAY TO TAKE INITIATIVE NAIMA.
I LOVE HIP HOP!
FLASHMOB EVERYONE! WHO'S READY TO DANCE?
SIT DOWN AILEEN!
YOU! OVER THERE. GIVE ME THAT.
GET THEM OUTTA HERE!!
IF I'VE LEARNED ANYTHING IN THE LAST DAY, IT'S THAT IN ORDER TO BE FREE WE NEED TO SEE THE POTENTIAL IN EVERYTHING!
SO I'M TELLING ALL OF OUR CUSTOMERS ON SCREEN TO--

HE'S GOT A GUN!
THAT'S JUST A NEFERTITI NECKLACE, CHRIS.
OH. NICE NECKLACE BRO! I LOVE ANGELINA JOLIE TOO!
TIME HAS COME Y'ALL!
THE ORIGINAL MAN IS BAAAAAACK!
IN SECTION 4.5 OF THE DIVERSITY INTERPRETATION CENTER FOR KINDNESS FEDERAL GRANT IT STATES, AND I QUOTE, "PROGRAMMING MUST BRIDGE THE GAP OF UNDERSTANDING BETWEEN MAINSTREAM AND UNDERREPRESENTED CULTURES."
AND ANCIENT EGYPT IS CLEARLY UNDERREPRESENTED! HA! THE TEACHER IS HERE! THANK US LATER.

GET OFF MY SISTER!!!!
THWACK!
THUD!
GET CLOSE TO
ME AND I'LL POKE YOUR
EYE OUT!

Y'ALL GOTTA GET OUTTA HERE NOW--THE COPS ARE COMING! *AND NOTHING GOOD COMES TO THOSE WHO WAIT FOR COPS.*
I THOUGHT YOU SAID WE SHOULD TAKE OUR FREEDOM NOW?
THERE'S NOTHING WRONG WITH FREEDOM NOW. EVER. BUT FREEDOM TAKES TIME. AND THAT'S SOMETHING YOU DON'T HAVE--
MISS. WITH THE RESPECT. I READ THE WHOLE FEDERAL GRANT. THERE'S SPACE TO TEACH OUR PEOPLE ANCIENT KEMETIC TRADITIONS. IT WILL HELP US GET FREE..
HOW CAN WE BE FREE IN A PLACE THAT NEVER INTENDED ON OUR SURVIVAL?

I CAN SHOW YA WHAT I MEAN. YA JUST HAVE TO WISH FOR THE RIGHT THING.
THANK YOU FAIRY! SINCE I DIDN'T GET MY LAST WISH, I WISH I HAD A TIME MACHINE. SO I COULD GO TO THE FUTURE!
THE PAST PLEASE. WHEN WE WERE KINGS.
THE PAST EXP
GOOD CHOICE HERE YA GO!
POOF!
IT'S A *BUS?* I TAKE THE BUS WAY TOO MUCH TO GET ON IT FOR LEISURE...
THIS WILL BE THE ONLY FAMILIAR THING YA GONNA SEE, SO BE THANKFUL! NOW GO ON.. GET ON THE BUS!
THE PAST EXPRESS

WAIT FOR ME!!
I HEARD YOU'RE GETTING A TIME MACHINE? AND YOU DIDN'T INVITE ME? AND YOU KNOW I LOVE THE OLDIES. DAMN.
HURRY UP. GET ON THE BUS!
FUTURE. HERE WE COME!
NAH SIS. YOU GOTTA KNOW THE PAST BEFORE YOU GO TO THE FUTURE. THINK ABOUT IT.
WE ARE NOT GOING BACK TO THE PAST. THE FUTURE IS THE ONLY HOPE FOR BLACK PEOPLE!!!
FLICK!
WOMP-WOMP-WOMP!!
GASP!
TO BE CONTINUED...
SCAN THE CODE OR GO TO SOUNDCLOUD.COM/HAFROCENTRIC TO LISTEN TO THE TIME MACHINE BUS

NAIMA HERE! THANKS FOR JOINING US ON THIS JOURNEY. IF YOU'D LIKE A GUIDE TO THE KEY CONCEPTS AND DISCUSSION POINTS OF (H)AFROCENTRIC, GO TO:

HAFROCENTRIC.COM

DOWNLOAD THE CURRICULUM BY SCANNING THE QR CODE!

TO GET IN CONTACT WITH NAIMA PEPPER,
TWEET HER @HAFROCENTRIC
INSTAGRAM.COM/HAFROCENTRIC
FACEBOOK.COM/HAFROCENTRIC
SOUNDCLOUD.COM/HAFROCENTRIC

HAFROCENTRIC.CO

THE ART OF
(H)AFROCENTRIC

Ronald Nelson '11

<- LEG MAYBE
TOO FAR OVER

STUDIES FOR (H)AF PROMO COVER

DIFFERENT EYE BROWS
NOSE IS NOT TURNED UP...
DIFFERENT FROM NAIMA (FULLER LIPS)
MAKE FACE A LITTLE SKINNIER

INCORDORATE MORE CIRCLES WHEN BUILDING THE 'FRO!
CURVE NOT POINT
NOTE!
PUT EAR HIGHER
I LIKE THIS BREAK
FULLER BOTTOM LIP THAN NAIMA

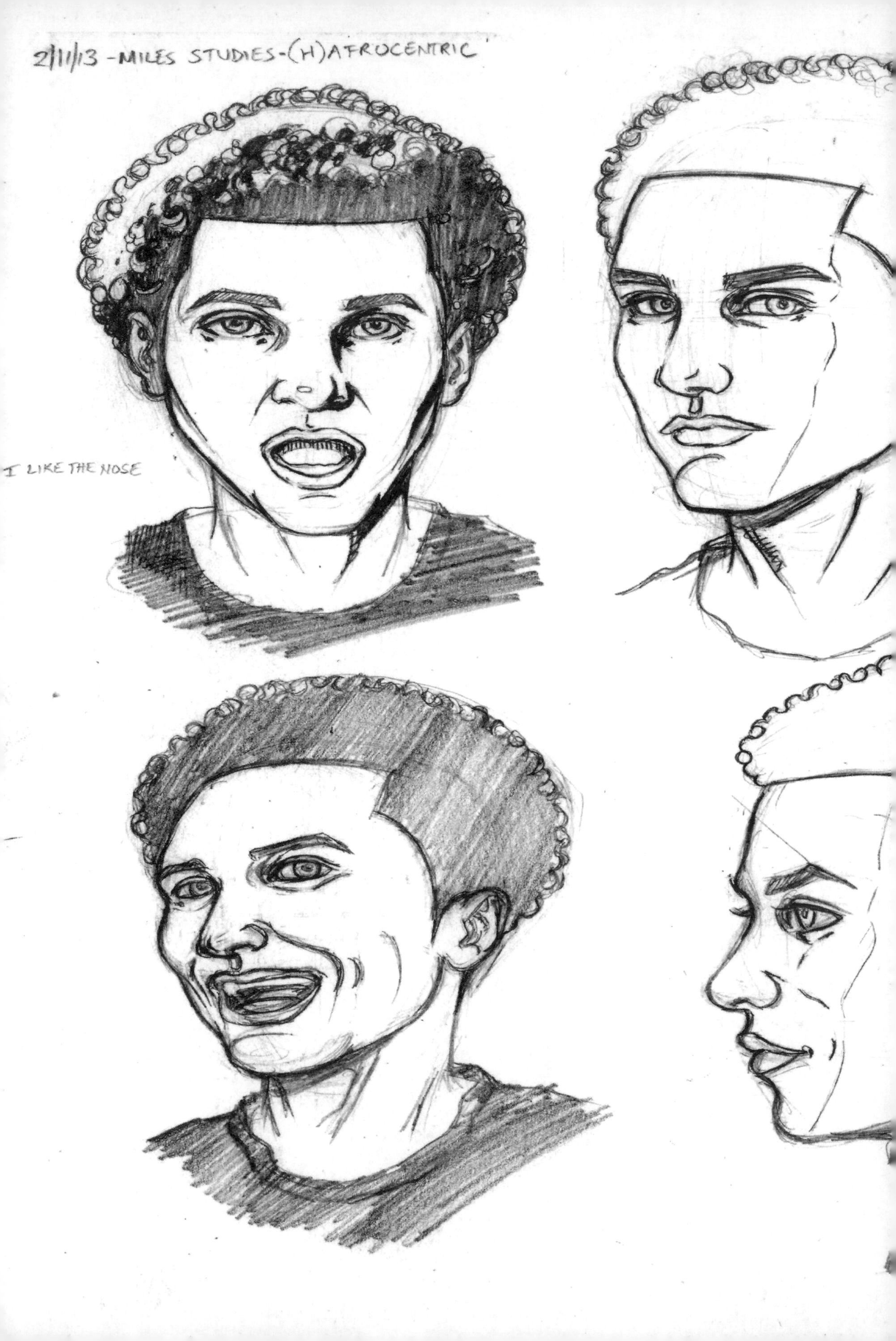
2/11/13 -MILES STUDIES-(H)AFROCENTRIC
I LIKE THE NOSE

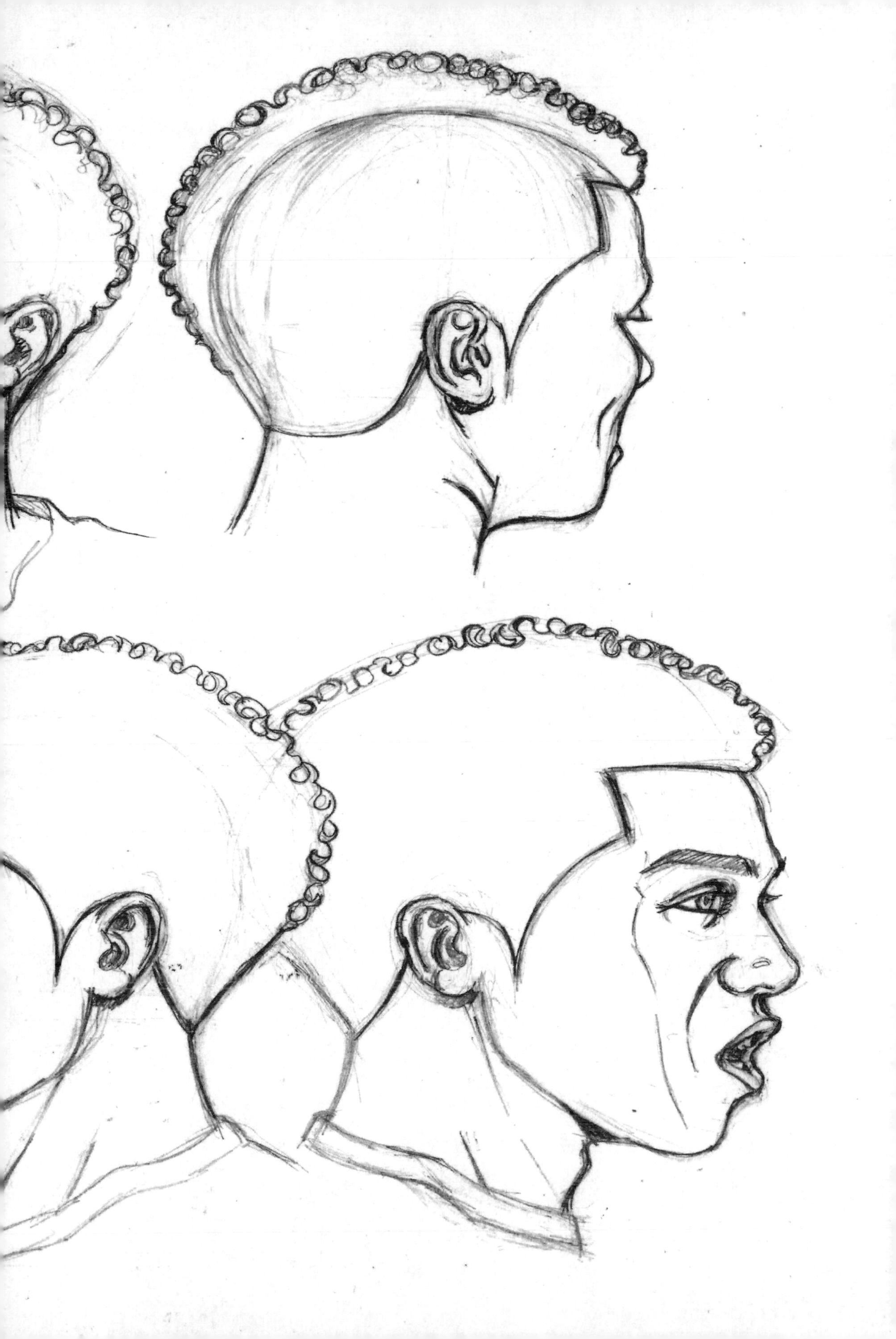

THE TEAM

Juliana “Jewels” Smith // Creator / Writer

Jewels is the creator and writer of *(H)afrocentric*. She won the Glyph Award for Best Writer on *(H)afrocentric Volume 4* and was honored by the African American Museum and Library at Oakland with the first annual Excellence in Comics and Graphic Novels Award. Smith has given talks about the relationship between comics, humor, racial justice, and gender equity at the Schomburg Center, New York Comic Con, Studio Museum of Harlem, Baltimore Book Festival, and The Cooper Union.

Ronald Nelson // Illustrator

Ronald Nelson is an illustrator and columnist from New York City. Recent exhibitions of his work have included the Adobe Art Center in Castro Valley and the Jazz Heritage Center in San Francisco. He’s created illustrations for various independent publishers and New York politicians, most notably Congressman Charles B. Rangel and Bronx Borough President Ruben Diaz Jr. As a columnist, he is regularly featured in articles for *The Amherst Bulletin*, *Amsterdam News*, *Daily Hampshire Gazette*, and *The Beacon*. Follow on Instagram @ronaldrobertnelson

Mike Hampton // Colorist / Letterist

Mike Hampton has been a self-published comic book artist and writer for over 10 years. Some of his titles include *Hot Zombie Chicks*, *Captain A-hole*, and his newest effort, *Eagle Eye & The Quail*. Mike has also lent his digital coloring talents to the popular indie comic *The Mustache Ride*, by Brandon Bracamonte, and *Won & Phil* by Age Scott. As a freelance graphic designer he has created logos, album covers, business cards, and fliers.

ABOUT PM PRESS

PM Press was founded at the end of 2007 by a small collection of folks with decades of publishing, media, and organizing experience. PM Press co-conspirators have published and distributed hundreds of books, pamphlets, CDs, and DVDs. Members of PM have founded enduring book fairs, spearheaded victorious tenant organizing campaigns, and worked closely with bookstores, academic conferences, and even rock bands to deliver political and challenging ideas to all walks of life. We're old enough to know what we're doing and young enough to know what's at stake.

We seek to create radical and stimulating fiction and non-fiction books, pamphlets, T-shirts, visual and audio materials to entertain, educate, and inspire you. We aim to distribute these through every available channel with every available technology—whether that means you are seeing anarchist classics at our bookfair stalls, reading our latest vegan cookbook at the café, downloading geeky fiction e-books, or digging new music and timely videos from our website.

PM Press is always on the lookout for talented and skilled volunteers, artists, activists, and writers to work with. If you have a great idea for a project or can contribute in some way, please get in touch.

PM Press
PO Box 23912
Oakland, CA 94623
www.pmpress.org

FRIENDS OF PM PRESS

These are indisputably momentous times—the financial system is melting down globally and the Empire is stumbling. Now more than ever there is a vital need for radical ideas.

In the years since its founding—and on a mere shoestring—PM Press has risen to the formidable challenge of publishing and distributing knowledge and entertainment for the struggles ahead. With over 300 releases to date, we have published an impressive and stimulating array of literature, art, music, politics, and culture. Using every available medium, we've succeeded in connecting those hungry for ideas and information to those putting them into practice.

Friends of PM allows you to directly help impact, amplify, and revitalize the discourse and actions of radical writers, filmmakers, and artists. It provides us with a stable foundation from which we can build upon our early successes and provides a much-needed subsidy for the materials that can't necessarily pay their own way. You can help make that happen—and receive every new title automatically delivered to your door once a month—by joining as a Friend of PM Press. And, we'll throw in a free T-shirt when you sign up.

Here are your options:

- **$30 a month** Get all books and pamphlets plus 50% discount on all webstore purchases
- **$40 a month** Get all PM Press releases (including CDs and DVDs) plus 50% discount on all webstore purchases
- **$100 a month** Superstar—Everything plus PM merchandise, free downloads, and 50% discount on all webstore purchases

For those who can't afford $30 or more a month, we have **Sustainer Rates** at $15, $10 and $5. Sustainers get a free PM Press T-shirt and a 50% discount on all purchases from our website.

Your Visa or Mastercard will be billed once a month, until you tell us to stop. Or until our efforts succeed in bringing the revolution around. Or the financial meltdown of Capital makes plastic redundant. Whichever comes first.

The Real Cost of Prisons Comix

Ellen Miller-Mack, Craig Gilmore, Lois Ahrens, Susan Willmarth, and Kevin Pyle

ISBN: 978-1-60486-034-4
$14.95 104 pages

Winner of the 2008 PASS Award (Prevention for a Safer Society) from the National Council on Crime and Delinquency

One out of every hundred adults in the U.S. is in prison. This book provides a crash course in what drives mass incarceration, the human and community costs, and how to stop the numbers from going even higher. This volume collects the three comic books published by the Real Cost of Prisons Project. The stories and statistical information in each comic book are thoroughly researched and documented.

Prison Town: Paying the Price tells the story of how the financing and site locations of prisons affects the people of rural communities in which prison are built. It also tells the story of how mass incarceration affects people of urban communities where the majority of incarcerated people come from.

Prisoners of the War on Drugs includes the history of the war on drugs, mandatory minimums, how racism creates harsher sentences for people of color, stories of how the war on drugs works against women, three strikes laws, obstacles to coming home after incarceration, and how mass incarceration destabilizes neighborhoods.

Prisoners of a Hard Life: Women and Their Children includes stories about women trapped by mandatory sentencing and the "costs" of incarceration for women and their families. Also included are alternatives to the present system, a glossary, and footnotes.

Over 125,000 copies of the comic books have been printed and more than 100,000 have been sent to people who are incarcerated, to their families, and to organizers and activists throughout the country. The book includes a chapter with descriptions of how the comix have been put to use in the work of organizers and activists in prison and in the "free world" by ESL teachers, high school teachers, college professors, students, and health care providers throughout the country. The demand for the comix is constant and the ways in which they are being used are inspiring.

"I cannot think of a better way to arouse the public to the cruelties of the prison system than to make this book widely available."
—Howard Zinn

Anarchy Comics: The Complete Collection

Edited by Jay Kinney

ISBN: 978-1-60486-531-8
$20.00 224 pages

Anarchy Comics: The Complete Collection brings together the legendary four issues of *Anarchy Comics* (1978–1986), the underground comic that melded anarchist politics with a punk sensibility, producing a riveting mix of satire, revolt, and artistic experimentation. This international anthology collects the comic stories of all thirty contributors from the U.S., Great Britain, France, Germany, Netherlands, Spain, and Canada.

In addition to the complete issues of *Anarchy Comics*, the anthology features previously unpublished work by Jay Kinney and Sharon Rudahl, along with a detailed introduction by Kinney, which traces the history of the comic he founded and provides entertaining anecdotes about the process of herding an international crowd of anarchistic cats.

Contributors include: Jay Kinney, Yves Frémion, Gerhard Seyfried, Sharon Rudahl, Steve Stiles, Donald Rooum, Paul Mavrides, Adam Cornford, Spain Rodriguez, Melinda Gebbie, Gilbert Shelton, Volny, John Burnham, Cliff Harper, Ruby Ray, Peter Pontiac, Marcel Trublin, Albo Helm, Steve Lafler, Gary Panter, Greg Irons, Dave Lester, Marion Lydebrooke, Matt Feazell, Pepe Moreno, Norman Dog, Zorca, R. Diggs (Harry Driggs), Harry Robins, and Byron Werner.

"*60s counterculture, supposedly political, mostly concerned itself with hedonism and self-focused individualism, as did the underground comix it engendered. Jay Kinney's and Paul Mavrides'* Anarchy Comics, *to which all the scene's most artistically and politically adventurous creators gravitated, was an almost singular exception. Combining a grasp of Anarchy's history and principles with a genuinely anarchic and experimental approach to the form itself,* Anarchy Comics *represents a blazing pinnacle of what the underground was, and what it could have been. A brave and brilliant collection.*"
—Alan Moore, celebrated comic writer and creator of *V for Vendetta*, *Watchmen*, *From Hell*, *The League of Extraordinary Gentlemen*, and numerous other comics and novels

"Anarchy Comics *was an education I never got in school. I learned more deep truths about the way human megatribes operate (while at the same time being greatly amused by the superb art and writing) than from any textbook. Decades later, the insights I gleaned from these brilliant comics still affect the way I view global events.*"
—Mark Frauenfelder, founder of boingboing.net

Understanding Jim Crow: Using Racist Memorabilia to Teach Tolerance and Promote Social Justice

David Pilgrim with a foreword by
Henry Louis Gates Jr.

ISBN: 978-1-62963-114-1
$19.95 208 pages

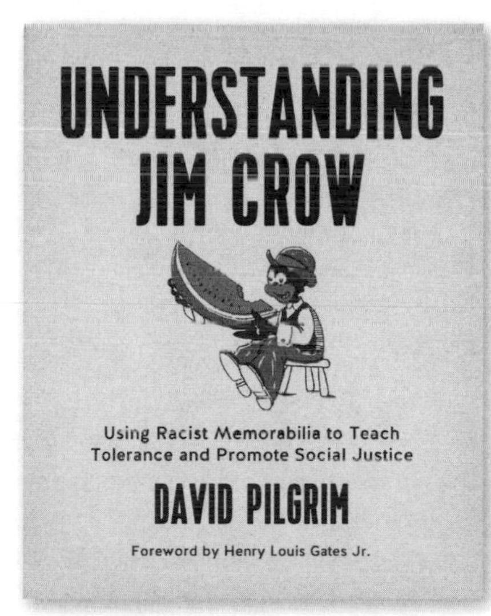
UNDERSTANDING
JIM CROW
Using Racist Memorabilia to Teach
Tolerance and Promote Social Justice
DAVID PILGRIM
Foreword by Henry Louis Gates Jr.

For many people, especially those who came of age after landmark civil rights legislation was passed, it is difficult to understand what it was like to be an African American living under Jim Crow segregation in the United States. Most young Americans have little or no knowledge about restrictive covenants, literacy tests, poll taxes, lynchings, and other oppressive features of the Jim Crow racial hierarchy. Even those who have some familiarity with the period may initially view racist segregation and injustices as mere relics of a distant, shameful past. A a proper understanding of race relations in this country must include a solid knowledge of Jim Crow—how it emerged, what it was like, how it ended, and its impact on the culture.

Understanding Jim Crow introduces readers to the Jim Crow Museum of Racist Memorabilia, a collection of more than ten thousand contemptible collectibles that are used to engage visitors in intense and intelligent discussions about race, race relations, and racism. The items are offensive. They were meant to be offensive. The items in the Jim Crow Museum served to dehumanize blacks and legitimized patterns of prejudice, discrimination, and segregation.

Using racist objects as teaching tools seems counterintuitive—and, quite frankly, needlessly risky. Many Americans are already apprehensive discussing race relations, especially in settings where their ideas are challenged. The museum and this book exist to help overcome our collective trepidation and reluctance to talk about race.

Fully illustrated, and with context provided by the museum's founder and director David Pilgrim, *Understanding Jim Crow* is both a grisly tour through America's past and an auspicious starting point for racial understanding and healing.

"One of the most important contributions to the study of American history that I have ever experienced."
—Henry Louis Gates Jr., director of the W.E.B. Du Bois Institute for African American Research

"This was a horrific time in our history, but it needs to be taught and seen and heard. This is very well done, very well done."
—Malaak Shabazz, daughter of Malcolm X and Betty Shabazz

Speaking OUT: Queer Youth in Focus

Rachelle Lee Smith, with a foreword by Candace Gingrich and an afterword by Graeme Taylor

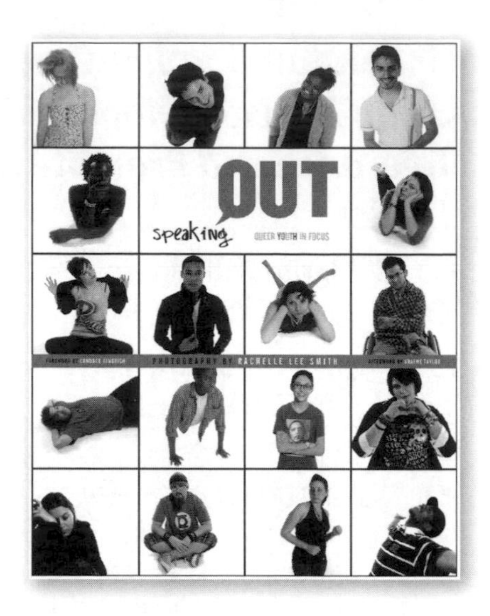

ISBN: 978-1-62963-041-0
$14.95 128 pages

Speaking OUT: Queer Youth in Focus is a photographic essay that explores a wide spectrum of experiences told from the perspective of a diverse group of young people, ages fourteen to twenty-four, identifying as queer (i.e., lesbian, gay, bisexual, transgender, or questioning). Portraits are presented without judgment or stereotype by eliminating environmental influence with a stark white backdrop. This backdrop acts as a blank canvas, where each subject's personal thoughts are handwritten onto the final photographic print. With more than sixty-five portraits photographed over a period of ten years, *Speaking OUT* provides rare insight into the passions, confusions, prejudices, joys, and sorrows felt by queer youth.

Speaking OUT gives a voice to an underserved group of people that are seldom heard and often silenced. The collaboration of image and first-person narrative serves to provide an outlet, show support, create dialogue, and help those who struggle. It not only shows unity within the LGBTQ community, but also commonalities regardless of age, race, gender, and sexual orientation.

With recent media attention and the success of initiatives such as the It Gets Better Project, resources for queer youth have grown. Still, a void exists which *Speaking OUT* directly addresses: this book is for youth, by youth.

Speaking OUT is an award-winning, nationally and internationally shown and published body of work. These images have been published in magazines such as the *Advocate*, *School Library Journal*, *Curve*, *Girlfriends*, and *Out*, and showcased by the Human Rights Campaign, National Public Radio, Public Television, and the U.S. Department of Education. The work continues to show in galleries, universities, youth centers, and churches around the world.

"Rachelle Lee Smith has created a book that is not only visually stunning but also gripping with powerful words and even more inspiring young people! This is an important work of art! I highly recommend buying it and sharing it!"
—Perez Hilton, blogger and television personality

"It's often said that our youth are our future. In the LGBT community, before they become the future we must help them survive today. This book showcases the diversity of creative imagination it takes to get us to tomorrow."
—Mark Segal, award-winning LGBT journalist

World War 3 Illustrated: 1979–2014

Edited by Peter Kuper and Seth Tobocman
with an introduction by Bill Ayers

ISBN: 978-1-60486-958-3
$29.95 320 pages

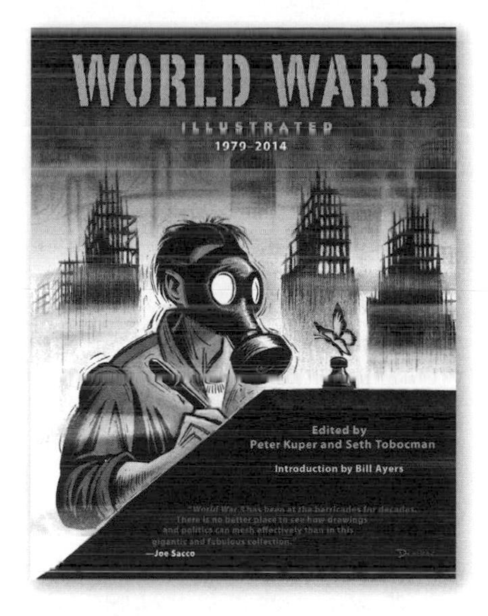

Founded in 1979 by Seth Tobocman and Peter Kuper, *World War 3 Illustrated* is a labor of love run by a collective of artists (both first-timers and established professionals) and political activists working with the unified goal of creating a home for political comics, graphics, and stirring personal stories. Their confrontational comics shine a little reality on the fantasy world of the American kleptocracy, and have inspired the developing popularity and recognition of comics as a respected art form.

This full-color retrospective exhibition is arranged thematically, including housing rights, feminism, environmental issues, religion, police brutality, globalization, and depictions of conflicts from the Middle East to the Midwest. *World War 3 Illustrated* isn't about a war that may happen; it's about the ongoing wars being waged around the world and on our very own doorsteps. *World War 3 Illustrated* also illuminates the war we wage on each other—and sometimes the one taking place in our own minds. *World War 3* artists have been covering the topics that matter for over 30 years, and they're just getting warmed up.

Contributors include Sue Coe, Eric Drooker, Fly, Sandy Jimenez, Sabrina Jones, Peter Kuper, Mac McGill, Kevin Pyle, Spain Rodriguez, Nicole Schulman, Seth Tobocman, Susan Willmarth, and dozens more.

"World War 3 Illustrated *is the real thing. . . . As always it mixes newcomers and veterans, emphasizes content over style (but has plenty of style), keeps that content accessible and critical, and pays its printers and distributors but no one else. If it had nothing more than that kind of dedication to recommend it, it would be invaluable. But it has much, much more."*
—*New York Times*

"Reading WW3 *is both a cleansing and an enraging experience. The graphics remind us how very serious the problems and how vile the institutions that cause them really are."*
—*Utne Reader*

"Powerful graphic art and comic strips from the engaged and enraged pens of urban artists. The subjects include poverty, war, homelessness and drugs; it's a poke in the eye from the dark side of America, tempered by what the artists describe as their 'oppositional optimism.'"
—*Whole Earth Review*

Revolutionary Women: A Book of Stencils

Queen of the Neighbourhood

ISBN: 978-1-60486-200-3
$14.00 128 pages

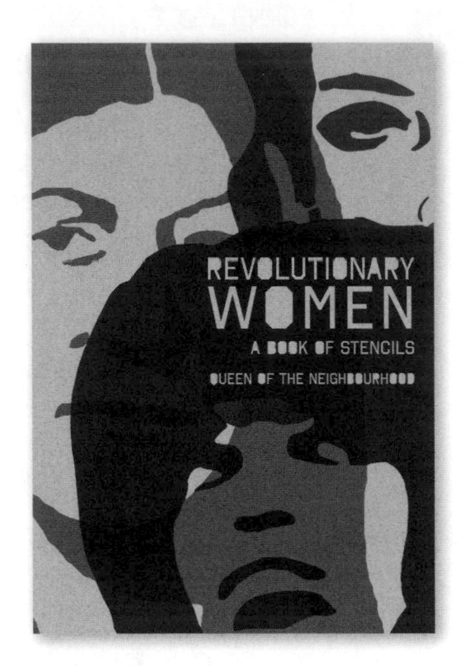

A radical feminist history and street art resource for inspired readers! This book combines short biographies with striking and usable stencil images of thirty women—activists, anarchists, feminists, freedom-fighters, and visionaries.

It offers a subversive portrait history which refuses to belittle the military prowess and revolutionary drive of women, whose violent resolves often shatter the archetype of woman-as-nurturer. It is also a celebration of some extremely brave women who have spent their lives fighting for what they believe in and rallying supporters in climates where a woman's authority is never taken as seriously as a man's. The text also shares some of each woman's ideologies, philosophies, struggles, and quiet humanity with quotes from their writings or speeches.

The women featured are: Harriet Tubman, Louise Michel, Vera Zasulich, Emma Goldman, Qiu Jin, Nora Connolly O'Brien, Lucia Sanchez Saornil, Angela Davis, Leila Khaled, Comandante Ramona, Phoolan Devi, Ani Pachen, Anna Mae Aquash, Hannie Schaft, Rosa Luxemburg, Brigitte Mohnhaupt, Lolita Lebrón, Djamila Bouhired, Malalai Joya, Vandana Shiva, Olive Morris, Assata Shakur, Sylvia Rivera, Haydée Santamaría, Marie Equi, Mother Jones, Doria Shafik, Ondina Peteani, Whina Cooper, and Lucy Parsons.

"*What you hold in your hands is a lethal weapon.* Revolutionary Women: A Book of Stencils *is a threat to the status quo and a dangerous wake-up call to every person who has ever dared to think for themselves.... I believe the words and art in this book have the power to mobilize a revolution. Rise up and let's join them now!*"
—Wendy-O Matik, author of *Redefining Our Relationships: Guidelines for Responsible Open Relationships*

"*This book cunningly uses the modern style of stencilling to make icons of some key figures in feminist movement. Readers are invited to spread their images across t-shirts, walls, and pavements to let the world know who really deserves to be remembered.*"
—Gareth Shute, author of *Hip Hop Music in Aotearoa*

"*The beauty and simplicity of message is stark in this zine. It is lovingly earnest with its handcrafted cut and pastes. The snippets are well-worded, the quotes cleverly chosen. The silhouettes of fearless females are striking. Overwhelmingly, one is left with a sense of the near universal absence of images of revolutionary women. From now on, every time I see a Che Guevara portrait, I will wonder about his many, unheralded and invisible sisters.*"
—Karlo Mila, author of *Dream Fish Floating*